JORDAN SONNENBLICK

SQUARE
FISH

SQUARE
FISH

An Imprint of Macmillan

Square Fish and the Square Fish logo are trademarks of Mamillan
and are used by Feiwel and Friends under license from Macmillan.

Library of Congress Cataloging-in-Publication Data
Sonnenblick, Jordan.
Dodger & me / by Jordan Sonnenblick.
  p.   cm.
Summary: Miserable because his only friend moved away and he has once again lost
a baseball game for his team, fifth-grader Willie Ryan's life suddenly becomes a lot
more interesting when he finds Dodger, a furry blue chimpanzee that only he can see,
and he has to decide what he really wishes for in life.
ISBN-13: 978-0-312-56122-2
ISBN-10: 0-312-56122-9
[1. Wishes—Fiction.   2. Genies—Fiction.   3. Friendship—Fiction.
4. Family life—Fiction.]   I. Title.   II. Title: Dodger and me.
PZ7.S69798Do   2008   [Fic]—dc22   2007032770

Originally published in the United States by Feiwel and Friends
Square Fish logo designed by Filomena Tuosto
First Square Fish Edition: March 2009
10 9 8 7 6 5 4 3 2 1
www.squarefishbooks.com

This book is dedicated to my mother, Dr. Carol Sonnenblick, who endured the gruesome spectacle of my Little League baseball career and never stopped cheering for me. I'm a big fan of yours too, Mom.

DODGER
AND ME

CHAPTER ONE

Willie Strikes Out

LOOK, IF I'M GOING TO TELL you everything that happened between me and Dodger, you have to promise you won't tell. And you won't laugh. And you won't mention any of this to dumb old Lizzie from England. I have a weird feeling she wouldn't appreciate it.

Not that I care what she thinks.

Anyway, I guess I'll have to trust you on this, right? Plus, I'm busting to tell somebody about it. So here goes.

It all started one Sunday afternoon on the baseball field. It was the second-to-last game of the fall Little League season. My team, the Bethlehem

Bulldogs, was losing 3–2 in the bottom of the seventh inning. In the ten- and eleven-year-old league, we only play seven-inning games, so this was it: We were coming up to bat for the whole enchilada. It was all or nothing, score or lose, the victory pizza party with the team or the PB&J at home with Mommy. Plus, the team was in first place, but we needed to win one of our last two games in order to finish the season as champions. There were two outs with runners on second and third when I stepped up to the plate.

Can you believe it? Me, Willie Ryan! The guy who had never gotten a hit all season. The kid who prayed to get hit by the ball just so he could get on base. Of anybody on the team, I should have been the LAST person you'd want batting in that situation. I'm serious: If you could have taken a vote of all the kids on my team, they would have agreed a hundred percent. They would have sent any other player out there in my place—even Joey Carbone, who had a broken leg. They would rather have sent my seven-year-old sister out there. Heck, if my grandma Lillian had shown up with regulation cleats on her feet, they would probably have wanted to bench me and send her up to bat. But instead they got me—and my team would lose if I didn't get to first.

By the way, not that it matters to me, but dumb old Lizzie from England was watching from the stands. And get this: She was cheering for me super-loudly as I approached the batter's box. I swear, when I grow up I'm going to invent a special portable soundproof booth for this exact situation. It will slide on special rails built into the bleachers at athletic fields, and it will have a detector built into it that picks up embarrassing cheering noises. So let's just say, for example, that there's a boy who doesn't particularly like girls, okay? And there's some girl who keeps following him around and showing up at his baseball games, even though it's totally unusual for a girl to show up at a boy's game in the first place, and completely unheard of for the girl to scream encouragement at one single player the whole game. Plus, the girl doesn't know a thing about baseball, so she keeps screaming the wrong thing at the wrong time. And let's imagine, for a moment, that the boy's whole team starts laughing at him even more than usual because they start to think he's in love with the girl. So they tell the boy stuff like, "Hey, you and Lizzie should get married. She's the only person in the world who doesn't know how much you stink!"

Well, anyway, if a thing like that happened, the booth would slide right over to the girl's seat, come down around her, and keep all of her humiliating sounds from reaching the field.

Since I didn't have a cheer-proof booth handy that day, I just had to stand there taking my practice swings and try to tune out the constant clapping and strange accented hooting noises that were coming from Lizzie. Right before the game, my little sister, Amy, had asked me, "Is that weird Lizzie going to be there? She sounds like a cross between a trained dolphin and a dodo bird. It gives me a headache!" Looking up into the stands as Lizzie's cheers reached their maximum level, I saw Amy holding her hands up near her face. It looked like maybe she was trying to shield her ears. Poor Amy. Poor me!

I stepped into the box and gave the pitcher my best glare. Unfortunately, because I have gigantic glasses and my mom makes me wear a special helmet with a mouth guard, he probably couldn't see my face at all. But he was glaring at me, too, and I could certainly see his face better than I wanted to. The kid was huge. I mean seriously huge. And tough. And old-looking. I knew he had to be my age, but if I'd seen him driving a motorcycle to the game, I wouldn't have been very surprised. Plus, he'd already gotten a warning for hitting two of my teammates with fastballs. I gulped and got into my stance. Now, I've spent hours and hours practicing my stance in the mirror, and I think it looks cool. But Amy says it makes me look like a praying mantis with arthritis.

Doesn't that girl have a great vocabulary?

Anyway, as the pitcher wound up, I did my best to stay calm and focused. When he let the ball fly, though, all I could *focus* on was the fact that the ball was streaking toward my head at about eighty miles per hour. I just barely had time to hit the dirt as the ball whistled by, about an inch above the top of my helmet. The catcher couldn't get his hands on the ball, and it went all the way to the backstop. My whole team started shouting to the guy on third, "GO! GO!" This was a perfect opportunity. He could steal home and tie the game without me having to actually hit the ball!

The runner, James Beeks, who happens to be the best athlete and the coolest kid in my fifth-grade class, hesitated for about half a second, and in that time, the umpire tried to step aside so the catcher could get to the ball. Then a lot happened at once. As I scrambled across the plate on my hands and knees to get out of the base path, James started to go. So did the guy on second. The catcher stretched his glove as far as he could along the ground. But just as the glove closed around the ball, the umpire accidentally stepped on it. The catcher yelped in pain and yanked his hand away. This made the ump fall backwards. The ball squirted free of the glove and rolled between the ump's outstretched feet. James was about five steps from the plate when the catcher finally managed to grab the ball bare-handed. The catcher lunged. He slapped the ball against the side of James's leg just as James's foot touched the corner of the plate, and as every Little Lea-guer knows, a tie goes to the runner. My whole team started jumping up and down, cheering and pounding each other on the back. It was a nice little moment for us.

Then the ump got up and called a meeting with the other umpire and both coaches. As the catcher took off his mitt and rubbed his crushed hand, and James walked slowly toward our dugout with his eyes on the huddled grown-ups, I stood there and thought, *If I ever needed a break, this is it. Please, please let the run count. I just need some help here.*

I guess there's a reason my nickname isn't Lucky, because the umpires ruled that the entire play after the ball hit the backstop didn't count. James started trudging back to third as our coach tried to calm the whole bench down. As I got back in the batter's box, James slapped me on the back and said, "All right, Wimpy, just bring me home."

That's another reason I can't be called Lucky: because everyone on the team already calls me Wimpy. The only guy who used to call me Willie was my best friend, Tim, and he moved to another state right at the start of the season. So now I was Wimpy one hundred percent of the time in the dugout, unless a coach was talking to me—and even the coaches sometimes almost slipped and used the nickname. Plus, even if the coaches weren't saying it, they were probably thinking it.

Back to the game: The count was one ball, no strikes. All I needed were three more terrifying pitches at my body and I'd get the walk. Then I could relax on first base and let the next guy worry about tying the game. The second pitch was nowhere near me, though. It was way outside, but the catcher managed to grab it before it could become another wild pitch.

Two balls, no strikes. The third pitch came screaming inside again, this time about an inch in front of my ribs. I stood my ground, mostly because my reflexes hadn't been fast enough for me to take another dive, and it was three balls, no strikes.

All I needed was one more ball. As I got ready for the fourth pitch, the catcher whispered menacingly to me, "Here it comes. . . ." And what came was a slow pitch, right down the middle. I had been waiting for another scary, wild fastball, so I didn't even manage to get the bat off my shoulder. Now the count was 3–1.

I swore to myself I would swing at the next pitch if it was anywhere close, just to prove I wasn't totally useless. That was a mistake: Apparently, I am totally useless, because the pitch was a little bit high, and I fouled it off for strike two.

I gave myself a little mental pep talk: *Come on, Willie. You knew it was all going to come down to you. One last pitch. One last chance. Now just get the good wood on it so we can all go get some pizza.*

The pitcher growled at me—I mean, he actually *growled*. Jeepers. The catcher mumbled, "Bye-bye, little guy!" And then the ball was coming straight over the plate so fast it looked like the pitcher had a cannon hidden up his sleeve. You have to give me some credit: I swung. Just as the ball smacked into the catcher's mitt with bone-crushing force, I sort of waved the bat through the space where the ball had been.

It was all over. The pitcher smirked at me, the catcher clutched his hand in pain, the runners on second and third moved slowly toward the dugout. In the stands, Lizzie was still shouting, "Yay, Willie!" while everybody around her just stared.

I tried not to listen to anything as my team

lined up to shake hands with our opponents. Most people just say "Good game, good game" about fifteen times as they walk past the other team, but believe me, there were some other comments being thrown my way that day. Life didn't get any better back in our dugout. I think the nicest thing anyone said to me was, "Geez, Wimpy, it was three and oh. You had him!"

Yeah, right. Like the pitcher had been practically on his knees at my feet, begging me not to destroy him with my mighty bat. Sure he had.

I got out of there as fast as I could, and got all the way to the stands before noticing that I still had my stupid ultra-safe batting helmet on my head. I whipped it off and spent a few moments trying to find my family in the crowd, but they weren't anywhere in sight. I suppose I wouldn't have wanted to be seen with me, either. Lizzie came up to me and said, "I'm sorry you didn't win, Willie. It looked as though you gave a great swipe at that last ball, though."

A great swipe, she said. Honestly. I just looked at her.

"Um, Willie," she continued, "your mum told

me to tell you that you'll have to ride home with me. Your sister just lost a tooth, and it was bleeding quite a lot, so your parents took her to your house."

Great. Only my parents would think their kid had to be rushed home because of a lost tooth. The good news was that at least they had missed the end of my horrible final at-bat.

Here came the bad news, straight from the mouth of Lizzie: "Willie, would you like to walk home together? My dad's supposed to drive both of us, but I could tell him to just drive on without us. I wouldn't mind at all."

Yeah, she wouldn't mind. And my teammates wouldn't mind having another reason to laugh at me. I needed to be alone, though. "Uh, I'm sorry, Lizzie, but I really need some time to think. So I'm just going to walk home alone, okay?"

She looked like I'd just smacked her, but she said, "Sure. I understand. See you tomorrow at school?" In case living on the same block with Lizzie wasn't enough, I was also in her class for the third year straight—and our moms were co-chairs of the PTA Safety Committee, so Lizzie even wound up at our house sometimes. Lizzie used to follow my old best friend, Tim, around all the time, but since he'd moved, she was always trying to hang out with me.

"Yeah. See you at school," I mumbled. Lizzie went to tell her father that I wasn't coming, and I started the long Loser Walk home. It's pretty amazing, really. If anything had gone differently—if my sister's tooth had stayed in her head for another hour, if Lizzie's dad had insisted on driving me, if good old Tim hadn't moved away, or even if Lizzie had convinced me to let her walk me home—I would never have met Dodger. Because that walk home changed my life.

CHAPTER TWO

A Meeting
in the Woods

MY HOUSE IS ABOUT EIGHT blocks away
from the baseball fields. You have to go straight
for four blocks, then make a right and go another
four blocks. There is a pretty big square of forest
in between, so the whole walk home is really a
walk around the edge of the woods. Now, of
course, going right up the middle would be a
much faster way, but those woods are a state
wildlife preserve. There are signs everywhere saying things like NO TRESPASSING and DO NOT LITTER
and PICK UP YOUR TRASH. There's some typical
grown-up thinking for you: If you're not allowed
to trespass in the woods, then how can you litter

13

there? And if you are not allowed to go there or litter, why would you need to pick up your trash? Finally, if you're the type who would trespass and litter in the first place, are you really going to be the kind of person who worries about picking up after yourself?

But anyway, of course kids cut through there all the time. My bedroom window looks out over the preserve, and even in the middle of the night I sometimes see strange lights and hear laughter in there. I never cut through those woods, though. My mom is too worried that I'll get kidnapped. Or catch West Nile virus, or Lyme disease, or tetanus. Or, heaven forbid, get a splinter. So on this day, I almost didn't go through the woods at all. But I felt like staying off the street so nobody could see me and talk to me about the pathetic game. Plus, if my mom hadn't deserted me, I would have been sitting in the air-conditioned comfort of our mini-van instead of baking in the hot sun all the way home, and the woods were always shady.

I stepped off the sidewalk, looked all around to make sure nobody was watching me, and slipped sideways into the forest. Sure enough, it was way

14

cooler in there. I even gave a little shiver as I paused to let my eyes adjust to the darkness under the trees. I knew there was a path that ran straight from the corner of the field to the corner of my block, because high-school kids used it to get to school every morning. I figured it should be less than fifty feet from where I had entered the woods, but I couldn't see anything that looked like a path at all. Under my feet was a thick layer of leaves and broken sticks, and I had to turn sideways every few feet to wiggle my way between thick, prickly bushes. I just kept telling myself that the trail had to be in front of me, but truthfully, I wasn't so sure. A couple of times I ran into big trees and had to skirt around them, which meant I was getting more and more turned around.

Panic rose up in my throat, and I felt like screaming. But that was just silly. I was still right near the ball field, so if I started shrieking like a kindergartner, whoever found me would have even more evidence that my name should be Wimpy. I gulped down some air, told myself not to be such a wuss, and stomped ahead.

Then I tramped around in there for fifteen solid minutes without seeing any sign of the path. This was ridiculous: The whole stupid forest was only four blocks on a side, so how could I have walked that long without hitting an edge? I sat down on a rock to think, but as soon as I stopped making noise, I started hearing lots of scary sounds all around me. First I noticed a constant buzzing that was probably coming from hives of killer bees. Then I tuned in to a whistling noise that was coming from either the wind in the trees or a vicious bear with asthma. Finally, there was a crunching sound off in the distance, which could have been a lot of things, none of them good.

The noises got me so freaked out that I put my dorky padded batting helmet back on to shield me from the sounds (and the bees and the wheezing bears). I panicked anyway and started running through the underbrush as fast as I could. Sticks and branches were ripping at my arms and legs, cold sweat was pouring down my face, and I wasn't even trying to pretend I had a plan anymore. Fear had completely taken over, and I was running for dear life.

To this day, I don't know how long my sprint lasted, but I know I didn't stop until I couldn't breathe anymore. I doubled over, put my hands on my knees, and gasped for air until I felt calmer. Then I straightened up and looked around. Without noticing, I had made my way into a sunny little clearing, which wasn't scary at all, just surprisingly blue. There was a bluebird singing from the top of a blueberry bush, and a little stream with clear blue water ran right through the middle of the sunniest patch and past some bluebell flowers before disappearing back into the forest. Only one thing ruined the entire scene: A crumpled red, yellow, and white fast-food bag was lying halfway in the water.

I was disgusted. Here was the only pretty place in the whole spooky forest, and some idiot had hiked in here just to dump his garbage smack-dab in the middle of it. I took a deep breath, sighed, and started to turn away. But then for some reason I stared at the paper bag in the stream some more. It was just so . . . wrong . . . that I couldn't stand to leave it there. Even though my mom has always warned me never to pick up trash from the ground, because "you never know *where* that thing has been," I walked over to the bag and lifted it slowly out of the water. The bottom was a soggy mess, and I was afraid it would rip, so I forced myself to slip one hand underneath. Now I was holding the bag just under my nose and started to feel a sneeze coming on. I noticed that there was some kind of blue pollen sprinkled all over the top side of the bag, so without thinking, I rubbed it off with my free hand.

All of a sudden, the bag started wriggling and bouncing around in my hands. I dropped it and jumped back. When I looked down, I could see that the bag was gone, and a strange-looking teapot was lying on its side in the grass. The teapot was swaying back and forth, and I had the terrifying thought that something was trying to fight its way out.

My terrifying thought was absolutely correct. As I watched, too scared to move, a furry blue hand shoved its way out of the pot's spout. The fingers clawed their way along the ground, and as they moved forward, they dragged an entire furry blue arm out of the spout behind them. Next came a painfully tilted furry blue neck and head, followed by another arm. As the arms began pushing downward on the ground, a hairy blue chest and stomach squeezed out of the teapot. At this point, I was staring at what appeared to be the upper half of a full-size, furry blue chimpanzee, which had somehow emerged from a teapot—a teapot that had somehow been a fast-food bag just moments before.

No wonder my mom always tells me the woods are bad news.

Just then the blue chimp-thing turned its head to look at me, and I saw that it was sporting a rather alarming black patch over its left eye. It was also talking to me. "Hey, bud," said the blue, patch-eyed chimp, "do you think I could maybe get a hand here? I'm sure this looks like a whole barrel of laughs to you but, dude, it's hard to squeeze through this little spouty thing."

Another thing my mom always tells me is that I should never talk to strangers. And no matter who else I'd ever met, this blue, one-eyed, chimp-in-a-teapot guy was stranger than all of them. In fact, he was so alarming I almost found myself wishing I had taken that ride home with Lizzie.

Almost.

I didn't know how to handle this situation, exactly, but my mom also always tells me I should be polite and helpful, even though it's hard to be polite and helpful if you're supposed to be afraid of everybody you meet. So I made my wobbly legs move until I was right in front of the chimp and reached a hand out to him. He grabbed on with one warm, rough, slimy hand and I pulled kind of gently. He looked at me like I was a wimp, which is of course true, and said, "Come on, dude, I don't have all day. I've been cramped up in this bottle long enough, and I'm pretty sure I'm sitting in a pile of cold, ketchupy french fries. So PULL!"

I pulled as hard as I could, and there was a popping noise, accompanied by a big smoky flash. The chimp let go of my hand, and I went tumbling backwards onto my butt. Then he stepped forward out of the smoke, and for the first time I could see all of him. He was about four feet tall and was wearing nothing but the eye patch and the world's loudest pair of orange-and-white surfer shorts. He held his hand out to me. "Sorry about that, bud, my grip must have slipped a little—I think there's some special sauce on my fingers." He stopped and licked his thumb. "Oh, dude, it is special sauce—OLD special sauce. Yuck!"

Great. If there's one thing worse than grabbing the hand of a scary, blue pirate-chimp, it's grabbing the mystery-sauce-coated hand of a scary, blue pirate-chimp. But he must have seen the disgusted look on my face, because he switched hands. This hand was dry, and he yanked me right up with no effort at all. "Hi," he said, "you must be Willie. I'm Dodger."

"Um, uh, hi," I replied. "How do you—"

"How do I know your name? Because, dude, I've been waiting for you to come and pick up my lamp." He grinned at me as he started picking what looked like little clumps of chicken nugget out of his fur and licking them off of his fingers.

"Lamp? You mean that little teapot thing? But

21

I didn't pick up the teapot; I picked up a fast-food bag."

"I know. That was a pretty smart disguise, don't you think? Three different kids passed through here just this morning, but not one of them even came close to picking up a soggy piece of litter. That's because you're the special one. You're the one who cares. You're the one who will be my new best friend!"

Okay, I was unpopular. But was I so amazingly unpopular that I needed a magical blue chimp for a best friend? Quite possibly. "Me? Are you sure you have the right kid?"

"If you're Willie Ryan, of Seven Lamplighter Lane, I have the right kid. And I have been waiting for you here for, like, a really long time."

"Uh, how long? Because that bag couldn't have been in the water for very long, or it would have fallen apart. Wouldn't it?"

He thought this over for a while as he stretched his long arms up over his head and twisted his waist back and forth. "I'm, uh, not really so good with time, dude. There's no clock in my lamp. But let's put it this way: I've waited ten thousand fries for you. I've waited nine hundred bags of ketchup. I've waited, like, fourteen Shamrock Shakes for you. So how long is fourteen Shamrock Shakes?"

"Well, I'm not sure. What's the last thing you remember?"

"Uh, do TV's have more than three channels yet?"

"Oh, man, Dodger. You *have* been in there a long time! But anyway, why would you wait for me? Why would you want me for a best friend?" As I said this, I couldn't help wondering, *Isn't there, like, a lonely blue surfer chimp somewhere that needs a buddy more than I do?*

"You're the one, Willie. I know you are. Didn't your best friend just leave you?"

"Uh, well, my friend Tim moved to—"

"Right, see? My best friend left me, too. And aren't you a really special guy who just needs a chance?"

"Well—"

"Me, too. And don't you like bananas?"

I had to think about that one for a minute. "Yes, actually. Now that you mention it, I do like bananas, Dodger."

"See, Willie? This is the beginning of a beautiful friendship."

Dodger reached behind him and tugged on the waistband of his shorts. Half of a sesame-seed bun rolled down his leg to the ground. Wow, I had a new best friend—a blue chimp with a burger wedgie.

CHAPTER THREE

Not out of the Woods Yet

JUST A FEW MOMENTS LATER, Dodger and I were walking through the forest on a path that had magically appeared right under my feet. I was carrying the teapot thing, and a thought suddenly hit me. I had rubbed the bag, and then it had become the teapot, and then a mysterious, impossible creature had popped out of it. Plus, the creature had referred to the thing as a "lamp." As crazy as the whole idea seemed, I had a weird hunch about my new friend.

"Dodger," I began, feeling like a complete idiot for even asking, "are you a, um . . . well . . . are you, by any chance, a genie?"

Dodger looked at me like I'd said a dirty word. Not that I'd ever do that, because my mom would probably have about three heart attacks if she heard me. Then he said, "Well, Willie, the preferred term is 'Bottled American.'"

"Okay, sorry. Are you a, um, Bottled American?"

Just then, Dodger waved his fingers through the air in a complicated little pattern, and all of a sudden we stepped out of the woods and into my backyard. "Hey, look," he said, "dude—we're home!"

Oh, boy. What was with the "we" stuff? Did Dodger plan to come into my house? Or worse, did he intend to *live* with me? My mom hadn't let me bring home the class hamster for a weekend in third grade—how was she going to react to having a talking blue surfer chimp with a vision problem in the guest room?

Just as I was about to ask him what, exactly, he meant by "home," he said, "Oh, man! I can't wait to get washed up and eat some fresh fruit! And then we can play games. And then we can make our Three-Part Plan. This is going to be so great!"

Three-Part Plan? What was he talking about? And why was he marching across my backyard toward our screen door in broad daylight? What if somebody saw him and called Animal Control? Or worse, *America's Funniest Home Videos*?

"Stop!" I shouted. "You can't just go barging in there. What if someone sees you?"

"Willie, has anyone ever told you that you worry too much? You need to chill or you're going to get high blood pressure before you hit middle school."

"But—"

"Buddy, it's all taken care of. Watch and learn, all right?" With that, Dodger turned the handle of the back door and stepped into the playroom of my house. I almost swore under my breath, but remembered just in time that I don't swear.

It crossed my mind that I was totally doomed. My mom was the type who would throw a fit and make me use about a gallon of hand sanitizer if I even touched anything at the petting zoo, and now I was barging into the house behind a talking blue chimp. I had no clue what to do about it, though, so I took a deep breath and followed him in.

27

He was standing about three feet from the door, looking around with total glee at all of the games and toys my sister and I had lying around, plus the shelves and bins full of additional stuff. I guess there wasn't a very wide range of leisure activities in a magic lamp. It was funny to watch—he kept hopping up and down, saying, "WOW! This is so COOL!" and then doing a little dance step. But it would have been funnier if I hadn't been waiting for my mom to come downstairs and freak out.

Then things got less funny in a hurry. Dodger started racing around the room touching everything and making happy chimp noises. He was juggling random objects—at one point, he had an old alphabet block, one of Amy's ice skates, and a book of sudoku puzzles all up in the air at once—while balancing my favorite model ship on his head. I was running around after him, trying to catch the toys he was dropping and making little shushing sounds, which he totally ignored. Finally, I shouted, "STOP IT!" just as my mom came barreling into the room to see what the commotion was. I jumped sideways so that I was between her and Dodger, as though an eighty-pound fifth grader could block the view of a 125-pound chimpanzee with a tall plastic ship on his head.

Sometimes with my mom, things go better if you don't wait for her to speak. So I jumped right in: "Mom, this isn't what you think! I mean, he just followed me home. He's not, uh, moving in with us or anything. Well, uh, he might be for a little while. But just until we get this whole magic lamp thing sorted out and all. Plus, he's much cleaner than he looks, and he has excellent taste in frien—"

My mom and Dodger both started shouting at the same time. Mom said, "What in the world are you talking about? WHAT isn't what I think? You should have been home half an hour ago! I've been worried sick—I was just about to call the police! And are you tracking ketchup all over our new rug?"

Dodger said, "CLEANER THAN HE LOOKS? What do you mean, cleaner than I look? I don't look clean? Dude, I am very well-groomed. Besides, YOU try being smushed up inside a stupid Happy Meal for ten years and see how spotless you come out!"

I turned from my mom to Dodger, then back to Mom. Then back to Dodger. I had no idea what to say. Finally, Dodger calmed down and gave me some helpful info that I wished he had shared a bit earlier: "Dude, I get it! You think your mom can see me, don't you? Oh, man! That's hilarious! No wonder you were, like, wetting your pants just now. I told you you should just chill. Watch this!"

I turned back to Mom, who was looking at me like I had just stepped out of a flying saucer. Dodger ran around behind her and started making weird faces at me while Mom started winding up for a big lecture: "I don't know what's gotten into you today, William. First you refuse a ride I'd arranged with Lizzie—her father called here right after your game. Then you wander around doing God knows what, until finally, I find you running in circles around the family room shouting at yourself!"

Dodger stood about an inch away from Mom's shoulder, reached into his mouth with both hands, and pulled his cheeks inside out. I had to try really hard not to laugh, but I managed.

Meanwhile, Mom was moving into high gear.

"You look at me when I talk to you, young man! I don't know where you got this crazy talk about someone moving in with us . . ."

Dodger let go of his face and started pretending he was polishing Mom's left earring. I ignored him.

". . . but there is clearly nobody else in this house. Your father is with your sister at the dentist, and I was upstairs cleaning. So unless you have a new invisible friend, please cut out the monkey business, take off your shoes, and start cleaning up whatever you've just gotten all over the rug."

Dodger looked straight at me and mouthed, *Monkey business?* Then he started hopping on one foot, scratching one armpit, and puffing his cheeks out like balloons. I couldn't help it: I burst out laughing.

Bad move. Mom got all offended. "You think this is funny, mister? I was sick with worry. It's bad enough that your sister is practically bleeding to death, but then I had to wonder where my little boy was, and—"

"Bleeding to death, Mom? Amy is bleeding to death?"

31

"Well, probably not, dear. But still—"

"Didn't she just lose a tooth—the one that she's been wiggling around all week? And isn't that totally normal?"

"Well, yes, but—"

"So how is that almost bleeding to death? I can't believe you sent her to the dentist because she lost a tooth. You exaggerate everything, Mom. I just took a little walk. I was in a bad mood, so I wanted to be alone." Just then, I noticed a little piece of twig poking my shoulder through my uniform jersey and brushed it away.

Mom noticed. "Is that a stick? It *is* a stick! Did you cut through the forest, William? You did, didn't you?"

Dodger was frantically shaking his head *NO*, but Mom basically had me busted, so I confessed.

"Yes, Mom."

"That is IT, William Ryan. I simply can't trust you anymore!"

I had never, ever answered back to my mom like this. Even so, I could tell that right about here is where I should have stopped answering and just let Mom wind down. But no, instead I just had to say, "Mom, you've never trusted me!" So that's why Dodger and I had to spend the rest of the day in my room.

Two hours later, with an hour left before dinner, I was bored and starving. It didn't help that Dodger reeked of fries, ketchup, and sesame seeds, so my whole room smelled like the drive-through lane of a fast-food joint. I was lying on my bed, fantasizing about pizza, steaks, and greasy fried chicken while Dodger blabbered on and on about my room, and how much better it was than the inside of his lamp. The actual blabbing dragged on with minor interruptions for maybe an hour, and went something like this:

"Dude. DUDE! I can't believe this is your room! It's so AWESOME! Wow, you must have twenty Yankee posters in here. You know, I met the fat one with all the home runs once. . . . I forget his name, but boy, did he like hot dogs. Anyway, this poster of the shortstop guy is so cool. And hey, I like this Yankee Stadium snow globe, too. Can I shake it? Oops. Sorry, man. But trust me—with a little water and some glue, that won't even be noticeable. Whoa! Are these your baseball cards? Hey, you forgot to open this pack from 1978 to get the gum out. May I? No? Whoopsie, too late. Man, don't get all bummed about it, I'll give you your half. What? Your mom doesn't let you chew gum? No wonder people think you're a wimp. I mean, well, you know. I don't think you're a wimp. But then again, I'm not a people, I'm a blue chimp.

"This room is just so great! Seriously. Did you know I once spent three decades in a Chinese takeout container? It was terrible—all the pork fried rice I could eat, for thirty thousand meals straight. Brutal, especially since I *really* prefer banana fried rice. All that salt made my fingers get bloated, too. Plus, all I had to read were the same four fortune-cookie fortunes over and over. When I got out, I smelled like duck sauce for a month, and all I could say for the first week was, 'Don't cry over spilt milk. Your lucky numbers are five, twelve, seventeen, thirty-one, forty-four, and forty-nine.' The kid who found me that time around played those numbers and won the lottery, though, which was kind of cool.

"And then there was the time I lived in a box of

doughnut holes. I had a ball in there. Get it? A *ball*? Because a doughnut hole is shaped like a ball. Oh, man, am I funny. . . . Are you even listening to me, dude? Yeah, sure you are. Anyway, living with the doughnut holes was *sweet* . . . get it? Sweet? Hey, are you falling *asleep*? Oh, man, I can't believe this. I think the little dude is asleep! Geez, maybe I can just wake him up with a little of the water from this snow globe. . . ."

You could say it was turning into a long afternoon. I had already blown a baseball game, and maybe my team's whole season. And now I was being followed by Dodger, who had already gotten me in big trouble with my mom and messed up my house. I was totally exhausted. But then I had an idea that gave me a burst of energy: "Hey, Dodger! When do we start with my wishes? I mean, I do get three wishes, right? Isn't that the deal?" Three wishes sounded like a good thing. Plus, and I hate to admit this, the sooner I made my wishes, the sooner the grease-soaked blue chimp would be gone. And maybe that could happen before my room got totally destroyed and my mom evicted me.

"Dude! You're awake! We can't, uh, do the wishes yet. In fact, if the Three-Part Plan works out the way it should, you won't even NEED wishes. *That* is the magic of ancient chimp wisdom."

"Um, you mentioned the Three-Part Plan before. But what is it?"

"Don't rush, buddy. Rushing around gives you indigestion. Plus, if we start in on the plan right away, we won't get to spend as much time just being pals. Right, pal?" He punched me playfully in the arm. I flew across the room, smashed into my 2000 World Series commemorative mirror, and slid to the floor amid a shower of glass shards. Great! Seven years of bad luck. I had a weird feeling my seven years had started earlier in the day, though.

Mom yelled from downstairs, "William Bennett Ryan, what was that crash?"

As Dodger mouthed *Bennett?* at me and giggled, I answered, "Nothing, Mom. Just getting thrown across the room by a blue chimp, that's all."

"Don't be a wise guy, mister. I don't *have* to feed you dinner, you know!"

As I groaned and slowly removed myself from the pile of razor-sharp objects that had been my favorite room decoration, I asked Dodger, "Okay, when can we start with this Three-Part Plan?"

"Soon," he replied with a sly little grin.

"How soon?"

"Not until the day after tomorrow, at the earliest."

"Uh, Dodger, why not sooner?"

"Well, little bud, before I can work my magic and fix up your life, first I have to observe you in your natural social environment."

A cold sweat instantly began dripping down my back. "What do you mean, my natural social environment?"

"Dude, tomorrow I'm coming with you—to school!"

CHAPTER FOUR

Mary Had a Little Lamb

YOU WOULDN'T BELIEVE how hard it is to get a chimp ready for school. I mean, first you have to teach it the names of all the colors, numbers, the alphabet . . . no, I'm kidding. What I really mean is that sneaking Dodger around the house, getting him food, and dealing with his bathroom needs were all really tricky tasks when both of my parents and Amy were all trying to get ready for their days at the same time. The worst was the bathroom. I had to dig up an extra toothbrush for him, and then he got all grumpy because it was decorated all over with pictures of the Little Mermaid. I pointed out that A) we were alone in the bathroom, B) he was invisible to everyone but me, anyway, and C) a girly toothbrush was way, way better than two-day-old monkey breath. Then I had to listen to a whole speech about chimps versus monkeys. Apparently, "Chimps are *so* not monkeys. We're great apes. So how's about showing some respect to your fellow primate? Besides, you better be thankful I'm not a monkey, buddy. I might have bad breath in the morning—but monkeys throw their poop to show displeasure. And I am not pleased with you right now. 'Monkey breath,' he says. Dude . . ."

And then there was the shower issue. I had to make mine super-quick so that Dodger could take one, too, without my family getting mad that I was hogging the bathroom. But then he complained the whole time he was in there. The soap wasn't fruit-scented. The shampoo wasn't bubbly enough. And we didn't have a back-scratcher he could use. A back-scratcher, for crying out loud. Then when he got out, he made me hand him my favorite towel, wrapped it around his waist, and marched out of the room—leaving me the horrendous task of scooping a wad of blue hair off of the drain.

But none of the morning rituals were half as scary as the idea of getting Dodger onto the school bus. It seemed to me that Dodger should just stay home, or maybe hang out in the woods all day. I mentioned this on our way downstairs for breakfast and he didn't say anything. Five minutes later he started talking to me about it, as I sat at the kitchen table, ate all-natural, unsweetened oatmeal with my family, and pretended I wasn't listening to an invisible primate. I just shoveled in my food, wished I could be eating sugary cereal like a normal kid, and tried to listen to my dad telling my mom about the work he had to do that day. Dad is an author. He writes self-help books about marriage, and he had to do some telephone interviews about the newest one, *Yes, Dear: Ten Things to Say to the Difficult Wife*.

Meanwhile, Dodger was getting himself psyched up for the day, too. "You think I can't handle the school bus? Dude, I'm a wild animal. I've faced the deadly black mamba snake. I've outrun a charging rhinoceros. I laugh in the face of danger. You think I'm going to go hide in the woods because a bunch of snotty little kids are too scary for me? I will get right on that bus! I will pound my chest with my fists! I will bellow my fierce cry of rage! I will . . ."

Jeepers, I'd rather hide in the woods than face dumb old Lizzie from England, but whatever. With my whole family sitting there, I couldn't answer him, anyway.

Twenty minutes later, Dodger was cowering under my seat, praying for the insanity to stop. As a gigantic ball of spit-moistened paper bounced off of his outstretched leg, I reached down there to give him a reassuring pat, and he grabbed my hand so hard I thought my bones would snap. Lizzie had gotten on at my stop, and her nonstop babbling could not have been helping. As usual, she had sat down next to me. Before my best friend, Tim, moved away, he'd always gotten on at our stop and been my human Lizzie shield—in fact, she had always talked a ton to him, but basically ignored me. Without him, though, I was totally defenseless. She was on a roll:

"Did you have fun doing your baseball yesterday? It was quite an exciting match. And I daresay you would have won if you had just hit that one ball a little straighter. Or, you know, if you hadn't completely missed the last one. But you tried hard, I could tell. I was proud of you, anyway. And when the dreadful people around me started booing and chanting, 'Yay, Wimpy,' I gave them several nasty looks. In fact, I think that's what stopped them joining in when everyone started throwing their food wrappers at you as you left the court. Oh, dear, I hadn't meant to tell you that last part. Anyway, I do hope my cheering drowned out some of the comments those ruffians were making."

Somehow, between the general screaming, the flying objects, the extreme bumpiness of the ride, and Lizzie's painful recap of my pathetic ball game, Dodger and I survived all the way to school. I waited for everyone else to get off the bus, then helped Dodger to get himself uncurled from underneath the seat. As I worked to untangle a ball of ABC gum from his shoulder hair, I asked Dodger what he thought of Lizzie. "I think you should probably marry her when you grow up," he said dreamily. "Her beautiful voice was the only thing that kept me from going completely crazy back there. Plus, she has cute ankles. Is she a good cook? Do you by any chance know whether she likes bananas? My mother always said you should never give your heart to a girl who doesn't like bananas!"

Whoa. I had a feeling Dodger wasn't going to like my first wish.

But he just didn't understand how embarrassing Lizzie was. Like the first time I ever saw her, in third grade. We were in the middle of a history lesson about Paul Revere's ride, and the teacher had us chanting, "The British are coming! The British are coming!" We were interrupted by a knock on the classroom door. In stepped the school counselor, with her hand on the shoulder of a girl who was wearing a bright red jacket. The counselor said, "Hello, third graders! Remember I told you you'd be getting a new classmate this week, all the way from England? Well, I'd like you to meet Elizabeth Barrett. I know you'll give her a nice warm welcome."

The new girl was beaming, and it occurred to me that she probably thought the whole "The British are coming" chant had been in her honor.

I started to smile at her, and so did Tim. But then James Beeks shouted, "Look out! She's a redcoat!" All the cool kids started shouting, "Redcoat! Redcoat!" and Lizzie's smile just crumpled. I didn't join the shouting, but I did stop smiling at Lizzie. In fact, the only person who made friends with Lizzie that whole day was Tim. He never did care what the cool kids thought.

But I did. One of my life's goals was to make sure the cool kids didn't notice me. And Lizzie just had this amazing talent for sticking out.

Anyway, Dodger and I made it into school with no problem, and before I knew it we were in my classroom, waiting for my teacher, Mrs. Starsky, to begin the first lesson of the day: our weekly spelling pretest. The kid next to me, Craig Flynn, had been held back in fifth grade and was built a lot like Dodger. That is, he was shaped roughly like a cinder block with arms and legs. He whispered at me, "Hey, Wimpy—did you study?" I had just enough time to wonder who in the world would study for a pretest before Mrs. Starsky began to read off the list. This week's words were all place names. As Dodger hooted, danced, and climbed along the radiators, I tried to focus on the words. Things went okay for a while, until I got stuck on the ninth word: Serengeti. I stared and stared at what I had written on my paper, but it just didn't look right. Dodger climbed across the classroom's hanging fluorescent lights and swung down next to my seat. "That one's wrong," he murmured in my ear. "It's S-E-R-E-N-G-H-E-T-T-I."

I dropped my pencil on purpose and bent down to get it so I could whisper to Dodger without anyone seeing me. "How do you know?" I asked.

"Dude, the Serengeti is in Africa. Of course I know how to spell a place that's, like, practically my neighborhood. Trust me."

I sat back up and changed my answer. To my horror, I noticed that Craig Flynn was looking at my paper. He quickly changed his answer, too. Then Mrs. Starsky announced the next word: Tanzania. Again, I stared and stared at my paper, as Dodger whispered, "T-A-N-N-S-Y-L-V-A-N-I-A." That sounded totally ridiculous, but Dodger muttered in my ear, "I'm FROM there! Would I spell my own country wrong?"

Mrs. S. told us to hand our papers in, and I

panicked. I changed my answer to Tannsylvania. To my horror, Craig copied my new answer, too. Then Dodger mumbled, "Oh, wait. Maybe I'm getting that confused with Transylvania. Ooh, you might not want to put that down, Willie."

I tried to change my paper again. Seeing what I was doing, Craig started frantically erasing his last answer, too. "Thanks, Dodger," I said. "Do you have any other brilliant ideas?"

"Look up," he hissed.

"I can't look it up, you . . . you . . . chimp! I have to hand in my paper!"

"No, LOOK UP, Willie!"

I did. Right into the furious glare of Mrs. Starsky. She snatched my paper off the desk and grabbed up Craig's, too.

"Well! I have never seen such a bold example of cheating—and on a pretest, for goodness' sake! What do you have to say for yourself, Mr. Ryan?"

"Uh, I wasn't cheating?"

"Oh, really?" she asked with her left eyebrow raised.

Don't you hate it when teachers get all sarcastic, by the way? I nodded.

She made a big show of comparing my paper with Craig's. "So there just happen to be two fifth graders in the world who think not only that Serengeti is spelled like 'spaghetti' but that Tanzania somehow rhymes with Pennsylvania?"

"Um, maybe?"

"And they just happen to sit next to each other?"

"Mrs. Starsky, I swear I didn't cheat."

Mrs. Starsky crossed her arms and started tapping her foot. Uh-oh. "You are making me really angry now, William. I know that you are a good speller. It's not like you to make these bizarre mistakes on your own. And I heard you whispering to Craig."

Oh, boy. How was I going to explain this? "Well, Mrs. Starsky, I wasn't actually talking to Craig. I was talking with my . . . uh . . ."

"Your what, William?"

I had to think fast. "Well, see, I have this, umm, imaginary friend. And I was asking my, umm, my friend for his—his—his imaginary eraser. And then—"

"I don't have time for this, William. Your grade

for the day is a zero. Also, I am writing a note home to your parents about your behavior. I will administer this test to both you and Craig first thing tomorrow morning. I'd suggest you study this evening—or bring a smarter imaginary friend tomorrow." She gestured with disgust at my paper. "A monkey could spell better than this!"

The whole class cracked up. In fact, I looked around, and the only ones in the whole room who weren't roaring with laughter were Mrs. Starsky, Craig, and me. And Dodger: I don't think he liked hearing that a monkey would do better than he did in *anything.* Ooh, I almost didn't notice, but there was one other person who wasn't laughing at me. I'll give you a hint: She used to live in England.

I sat there fuming through the rest of language arts and all of math, while Dodger took a nap under the art table in back of the room and Craig glared at me. When lunchtime came, I sat at a table in a shadowy corner of the cafeteria. While everyone else waited in the hot-lunch line for pizza and fries, I took out my usual embarrassing health-food lunch: a slice of wheat bread, a health-food fruit bar, and a thermos of soup. All I wanted was to be alone. Of course, I nearly got my wish. Nobody but Dodger wanted to be anywhere near me—except Lizzie. There was only room for two little plastic seats at the table. Of course, I was at one. Dodger tried to sit at the other. It was pretty funny: He was about twice as wide as the chair and had to balance by reaching his long arms down and putting the backs of his knuckles on the floor. That totally didn't work, so he stood back up and I dragged his chair to another table. Then he squatted on the floor, which looked a lot more comfortable for him. Lizzie saw there was space at my table and came zooming over like a rocket, grabbing an empty chair on the way.

"Hey," she said, "I'm sorry about this morning. Mrs. Starsky was being dreadfully unfair. Although you probably shouldn't have made up that excuse about the imaginary friend." Then she swung the chair in next to me, smacking Dodger's kneecap in the process. He hopped around in little circles and grunted while Lizzie started unpacking her bag lunch. Dodger got himself back under control in time to gaze longingly at the banana yogurt she took out.

I said, "Yeah, well . . ." because my general Lizzie strategy is to speak to her as little as possible. I keep thinking she will speak less in return, but things haven't worked out that way so far.

She responded by making a speech about how Mrs. Starsky was trampling on my rights as an American. I mostly tuned her out, looking around the room, nodding once in a while so she'd think I was listening. But then her tone changed all of a sudden, and I kind of woke up. "Hey!" she squealed. "My yogurt!" Suddenly I noticed that the table was covered in yogurt. Lizzie was covered in yogurt. And there were little droplets of yogurt in my hair.

Right in front of where Dodger had been kneeling, the bottom third of a yogurt container was lying on its side. The top two-thirds of the container was standing upside down next to it. There were jagged teeth marks all along the edges of each. I looked at Dodger, whose entire face was dripping with yogurt goo. "Oops!" he said. "I never *did* get the hang of all these silly plastic containers."

Lizzie just sat there, stupefied. I whispered, "Dodger! Hide!"

"Why?" he asked. "You're the only one who can see me."

"Uh, yeah, but I think other people might be able to see a floating mess of yogurt."

Poof! Just like that, Dodger disappeared. Lizzie, who had started frantically dabbing at herself with a wad of napkins, stopped long enough to ask me, "Did you just say something?"

"Uh, no," I said. "How did you manage to splash all this yogurt everywhere, Lizzie? Didn't they teach you how to eat in England?"

Lizzie said, "Of course they taught me how to eat! How could you . . . I . . . you . . . ugh! And to think I came over here to be nice to you!" Then her eyes started to fill up with tears and she ran out of the lunchroom.

I sighed and unscrewed the cap of my soup thermos. With a wet *POP!*, Dodger appeared next to me, jumping up and down and fanning himself. The yogurt was off his face, but it had been replaced by little bits of—I sniffed at the air—chicken soup.

Apparently, when I'd told Dodger to hide, he had decided to conceal himself in my lunch.

"Ooh, it's HOT in there!" he exclaimed. "I haven't felt anything like it since those Aztecs sacrificed me and my third master to their angry volcano god back in—hey, where's Lizzie?"

"She ran away crying."

"Well, that went rather well, Willie."

"What do you mean, that went rather well? Didn't you just hear me say she ran away crying?"

"Dude, of course I heard you. We chimps have excellent hearing, sharpened by thousands of years of—"

"Yeah, but didn't you HEAR ME? We just made Lizzie cry."

"Right. And I happen to know that your first wish was going to be: 'Make Lizzie stay away from me.' Wasn't it?"

"Well, sure. But—" I had admit, he was right. And I had wanted to make her go away. But for some reason, I felt kind of rotten now that I had done it. Even if she was super-annoying.

"But nothing. She's away, isn't she?"

"Yes, but—"

"Stop saying 'but,' okay? I like Lizzie. And that yogurt was excellent! But I'm just doing what you want me to do. If you want to drive away the one person in this school who cares what happens to you, it's none of my business. Now I have to go to the first-grade tables. Some kid over there brought a huge bag of mixed-fruit roll-ups. Yum!"

He went bounding across the room. Just as the high-pitched screams of the first graders began to fill the air, I decided I had better eat the rest of my lunch and try to get the table (and my hair) cleaned up a bit before Mrs. Starsky came for us. I plunged my plastic spoon deep into my soup, then stuck it in my mouth—and spat the entire mouthful across the table.

A note to the reader: Chicken soup tastes better if it's not mixed with banana yogurt and chimp hair. Just as I was about to get up and go dump out the rest of the muck that had been my lunch, a shadow fell over me. I looked up and saw the lunch lady standing over me, snarling. One of her hands held a dripping, stinky mop. The other was clenched tightly around the upper arm of my crying former lunch companion, Lizzie.

Then, over the wailing of what sounded like the entire first grade, plus one hungry chimp, I heard the enraged voice of Mrs. Starsky saying, "What in the world is going on here?"

All in all, it was turning into a pretty long day.

CHAPTER FIVE

The Home Front

DODGER REFUSED TO GET BACK on the
school bus, and I was in no hurry to get home with
my note from Mrs. Starsky, so we took a long walk
after school. You could probably guess that I was
in a bad mood, but Dodger was really on a ram-
page:

"That teacher of yours is *nuts*. Get a smarter
imaginary friend, she says. She thinks I'm dumber
than a monkey. Just because I'm a little bit rusty
in the spelling department. A smarter imaginary
friend? Hmph!"

"Uh, Dodger? No offense, but Mrs. Starsky
doesn't even believe I *have* an imaginary friend.

She was just being sarcastic. She really thinks I was cheating with Craig."

"Oh, great, Willie. You're saying she thinks I'm so imaginary that I'm not even *really* imaginary?"

"Dodger, this isn't about you. It's about how this was the worst school day of my life. And how my mom is going to kill me."

"Dude, funny you should mention that. Because it's time to start working on Part Two of the Three-Part Plan. . . ."

By the time we walked in my front door, I was basically terrified. I now knew two parts of Dodger's plan. The first was to "solve your Lizzie problem," and the second was to make my mom stop being so overprotective. Dodger still wouldn't tell me the third part, but I was having trouble imagining how it could be worse than the first two.

Silly me. Looking back, I should have imagined a little harder.

Naturally, as soon as my mom read Mrs. Starsky's note, she sent me to my room until dinner, with strict orders to study my spelling words. She also warned me that I should "Just WAIT until your father gets home, young man!" So I was a little nervous, and being nervous made it hard to study. So did Dodger.

"Dude," he said as soon as I sat down at my desk with my spelling book, "you're going to spend the whole night in your room, anyway—we might as well play for a while before you look at those words."

"What do you mean, the whole night? My mom just said until dinner, not the whole night."

"Trust me, Willie. Things happen."

Oh, that was excellent news. I asked Dodger to leave me alone for a while, which made him get all huffy. But he went *POOF* and disappeared. I forced myself to go over the words. I even wrote them five times each. It didn't take long for me to become an expert on S-e-r-e-n-g-e-t-i and T-a-n-z-a-n-i-a. Then I had nothing to do. I tried playing games on my handheld system, but Mom heard the beeps, came in, and confiscated my toy. I tried reading, but I was too hyper. Finally I said, "Dodger—come back!" I felt kind of dumb talking to the air, but didn't know what else to do.

I waited. Nothing happened. I raised my voice and tried again.

Still nothing.

I tried one last time, almost shouting it. Dodger didn't magically appear, but my sister, Amy, did, popping into my room without knocking, as usual. "Who are you talking to, Willie?"

"Nobody. I'm just studying my spelling words. Sometimes I like to say them out loud."

"Yeah, right," Amy said with a seven-year-old sneer. "You're up to something, and I'm going to find out what. I'm on to you, buster!" Then she stomped out. I swear, sometimes it was like she was my mom's clone or something. And one of my mom was already too much for me.

As soon as I heard Amy's footsteps fading down the stairs, I had an idea. It killed me to do it, but I said, "Dodger, *please* come back!"

Poof. Dodger appeared. "Hey, bud," he said. "I knew you'd miss me. Wanna play fear-ball?"

Fear-ball? What the heck was fear-ball? It was hard to believe I had actually asked Dodger to come back, especially when he explained fear-ball to me. The object of the game was to fix what

Dodger saw as the root of my baseball problem. He said I was afraid of the ball. Part Three of his plan was to make me a better ballplayer by conquering my fear. And the way to do that was to throw balls at me.

Fear-ball was dodgeball without the dodging part.

I tried to get out of the situation by suggesting other activities. But we couldn't play Trivial Pursuit because Dodger felt that spending years on end in a bottle gave him a disadvantage when it came to keeping up with the news. He refused to play chess because he said the horse-shaped pieces were degrading to animals. I offered to read to him, but he said, "Human books? Ha! Like what? *Clifford the Big Red Dog*? Have you ever tried to have a serious discussion with a dog? You might as well be talking to a tree—a tree that has an annoying habit of slobbering all over your fur. *Charlotte's Web*? Oh, because spiders are such great role models—except for the part where the females EAT the males. *Curious George*? At least he has opposable thumbs—but *please*. Dude, where's the chimp literature? There was this one book that my last master read to me called *Chimpy and the Chocolate Factory*. Do you know that one? About a kind, honest young chimp who finds a golden ticket and—"

I had to interrupt. "Uh, Dodger, I know that book. But it's not about a chimp. It's called *Charlie and the Chocolate Factory*."

Dodger looked heartbroken. "Oh," he muttered. "Oh."

Then he grabbed a Nerf ball from the corner near my closet and whipped it at my head. Nobody knows how to change a subject like Dodger.

Fear-ball wasn't very fun for me, although Dodger seemed to enjoy it. The game went like this: I would stand in front of my bed, after piling up a bunch of pillows on it. Dodger would grab one of the various balls that were scattered around the bottom of the old toy bucket in my closet. Then he'd instruct me not to move, and try to throw the ball as close as possible to my body without actually hitting me. He also said he'd start out with throws that weren't very close or very fast, but that each throw would be faster and closer. For the first ten throws or so, I flinched, ducked, whimpered, dived, etc. Then I started to have some confidence, some nerve, some guts. After fifteen throws or so, I didn't even blink until the ball whacked into the pile of pillows. Dodger announced that we were playing to fifty. I shuddered. At around the fortieth ball, Dodger took a couple of steps back, so that he was as far from me as the room allowed, and really started whizzing the balls by me. In fact, I was pretty sure the forty-fourth had grazed my right elbow. But I made it through to the last throw with all of my parts in one piece.

"Here goes, my fearless young friend. The final throw! And then you will be the new World Fear-ball Champion (Human Youth Division)! For this, we must add to the challenge. I want you to hold these weights!" He made me straighten my arms out to both sides, and put a notebook in each of my hands. "Now I want you to close your eyes. No, wait—that's not good enough. Here, try this!" He went into my closet and took the belt off of my bathrobe, tossing the robe to the floor in a heap. Then he wrapped the belt around my head so it covered my eyes and tied it tightly behind my head. Then I heard him walking away from me and picking something up from the floor.

"Uh, Dodger?" I asked shakily. "You're using a Nerf ball for this one, right?"

"Well, basically," he replied.

"What do you mean, 'basically'?"

"Well, it's a ball. . . . Now get ready!"

How was I supposed to get ready—make a last request? Watch my life flash before my eyes? I figured if I was going to get beaned, it might as well happen quickly, because my arms were starting to tremble under the weight of the notebooks. "All right, Dodger," I forced myself to say in the deepest, steadiest voice I could manage, "I was *born* ready!"

I felt every muscle in my body tense up, awaiting the sharp, sickening *THWACK!* of impact. I heard a swish and a creak that must have been Dodger winding up. Then, just when I knew the ball must be about to fly, I heard my mom pound on the door. "Dinner!" she shouted.

And that's when Dodger released the ball.

When I woke up, my mother was kneeling over me, holding the belt from my bathrobe and

screaming my name. It took me a moment to figure out where I was, and another moment to realize what must have happened. The throbbing
agony in the center of my forehead was the big
clue: Dodger had missed. Or not missed, depend-
ing on how you looked at it. He was standing behind Mom, peering anxiously over her shoulder at
me. I put my hand to my head and could feel some
kind of weird indentation lines crisscrossing about
two inches above the bridge of my nose. Over
Mom's wailing, I heard Dodger say, "Oops! Sorry
about that, dude. It's this eye patch—messes up
my depth perception. But man, you should have
seen it: a perfect spiral. It was like, *bang!* And then
you were like, ugh! And your mom was totally—"

I let my head ease back to the floor. Amy and
my dad came bounding into the room way too
fast. Amy tripped over Dodger's foot and crashed
into Mom's back. Then Dad tripped over the football that was lying there and crashed into Amy's
back. I watched in horror as all three of them
tipped forward onto me. By the time we got un-
tangled, Mom was scolding everyone in sight, Dad
was helping me to my feet and looking sheepish,

Dodger was hiding in the corner under my bathrobe, and Amy was cracking up while pointing at my forehead.

When my mom paused for breath, I asked Amy, "What? What's so funny?"

She couldn't stop laughing, but she did manage to hold her hands in front of her so that her two pointer fingers made a plus sign. I looked at her. I looked at the football. I looked at Dodger, or at least the blue bottoms of his feet sticking out from under the robe. I felt my forehead again. Then I dashed out of my room and down the hall to the bathroom. I hit the light switch and looked in the mirror. What I saw was horrible: Dodger had pegged me smack-dab in the middle of my forehead with the point of the football, where the seams meet. The impact had left a perfectly formed, bright red plus sign dented into my skin. I looked like what Harry Potter would have looked like if Lord Voldemort had been really into math.

Jeepers. This was no good at all.

I trudged back to my room, feeling sort of woozy from the impact of the ball, followed by the impact of my family. When I walked in with one hand covering my forehead, everyone started in on me. My mom said, in that icy-cold voice moms use when they're just on the edge of a total melt-down, "William, what exactly happened to you?"

"Well, uh, I was trying to use that belt"—she was still holding the belt from my robe—"to make a catapult. Um, for science? It's, like, this project-type thing, and—"

"A catapult? IN YOUR ROOM? William Ryan, why don't you ever use your head?"

Amy couldn't resist: "He did, Mom! Didn't you see?"

Dad looked like he was trying hard not to smile at that until Mom turned to him and said, "James, tell William that we won't tolerate this kind of behavior! He could have been severely injured."

Dad gave me a weak little shrug, but said, "William, we won't tolerate this kind of behavior! You could have been severely injured!"

"But Dad, I wasn't severely injured. I just got banged up a little. I'm fine, really."

Mom still looked upset, but now she focused on my injury. Gently, but forcefully, she pulled my hand away from my head. Amy snickered and said, "Wow, Willie, that's some addition!" I just looked at her. She snorted. "Addition—get it? Wow, I am definitely the funniest kid in second grade!"

And I was definitely going to be the dorkiest-looking kid in fifth grade.

CHAPTER SIX

Two Birds
with One Stone

SCHOOL THE NEXT DAY wasn't nearly as bad
as I'd thought it would be, even though everyone
looked at me funny because of my forehead. The
plus sign had turned a lovely shade of purple
overnight, which made it stand out even more than
it had the night before. But nobody asked me
about it directly except Lizzie. When she got on
the bus, she asked whether it hurt, and when I
said it didn't, she blurted out, "Well, that's a
plus!" Then she realized what she had said and
blushed. In fact, she was so embarrassed that she
didn't talk to me the whole day.

So that was half of the good news. The other half

was that Dodger had stayed home. He could barely look me in the eye after beaning me with the football, and insisted that he needed the whole day by himself so he could set up something super-special for after school. I admit that the thought of what Dodger could do with an entire day of planning was pretty scary, but at least it kept him away so I could get through school without getting in any more trouble. Craig and I both got hundreds on Mrs. Starsky's pretest-retest. Or re-pretest. Or pre-retest. Whatever you called it, I was relieved.

At lunch I sat at my usual table, alone. But with no Lizzie to bug me and no blue hair in my soup, I told myself it wasn't so bad. The afternoon went by quickly, because we were planting terrariums. I love terrariums, especially the good kind with real worms in them. And in fact, our homework was to bring something to put in our terrarium. Mrs. Starsky even gave each kid a little plastic jar. Which meant I could dig for some nice, juicy worms on the way home. Five minutes before the end of school, I was in a great mood. Then a monitor came in with a note. Mrs. Starsky called me and Lizzie to the front of the room.

There went the mood.

The note said that my mom and Lizzie's mom had to meet to discuss the work of their PTA committee at my house, so we should walk home together. "Take your time, and feel free to play outside on the way," the note said. Clearly, that was the work of Lizzie's mother; my mom's worst fear was what I could do to myself if I had free time to play. Rubbing my forehead, I could almost see her point.

When school let out, I started walking as fast as I could. Lizzie practically had to run to keep up. But then, just as we got to the place where the Little League fields ended and the edge of the forest began, I had to slow down. I couldn't believe my eyes: Half of the sidewalk was blocked by a hand-painted wooden sign on a homemade stand:

THIS WAY
4 WORMZ!!!

I stepped around the sign, just as Lizzie caught up with me. I had a bad feeling the sign was Dodger's work. First of all, the lettering was blue.

Second of all, who else would misspell "worms"? I just thanked my lucky stars that Lizzie wouldn't be able to see the sign, and started walking even faster. I noticed I was pulling away from Lizzie again. Looking back, I was happy to see that she had stopped to pick up some litter from the sidewalk. It looked like a red, yellow, and white fastfood bag.

Oh, no, I thought. *But it can't be. It just can't.* I turned and walked even faster.

About ten feet later, with a pretty loud *POP,* another sign appeared right in front of me:

HAY! YU MIST
THE WORMZ!

Again I stepped around the sign. This time I broke into a jog, thinking I could just run the rest of the way home. But the next sign popped up so close to me that I crashed into it and had to step back to read it:

TERN AROUND!!!

I did, and saw Lizzie standing behind me with her arms crossed, looking annoyed. She said, "Why are you running? Aren't you curious about these weird signs?"

Jeepers, I thought, *she can't see the signs, can she?* With a *POP,* one more sign appeared over Lizzie's shoulder:

YES, SHEE CAN!
SHEE PICKD UP THE BAGG TOO!

I sighed. This was too much. I knew Dodger had tested me with the litter trick. But just because Lizzie picked up a stupid paper bag, that didn't make her special.

Did it?

A bright blue carpet appeared right between me and Lizzie, and unrolled itself so that it became a path into the woods. I started to turn away from it, but Lizzie's voice stopped me: "Oh, come on, Willie. Don't you want to see what this is all about? We can have an adventure together!"

Oh, yay, I thought. *An adventure with Lizzie!* But

as she stepped happily onto the carpet and started skipping into the forest, I followed. Who knew what trouble Dodger and Lizzie could make for me if I let them have time alone together?

I caught up to Lizzie a few feet beyond the tree line. She smiled at me. "Isn't this delightful?" she asked. "Worms, a mystery, and a friend to share them with—what could be better?"

I almost choked. We walked side by side for a few minutes, until suddenly we were in a clearing. A blue clearing. Only this time, instead of a little blue clearing with a stream, it was a huge blue clearing with an entire blue baseball field in it, and thick, dense bushes all around. In fact, as we stepped off of the carpet, the bushes closed behind us so that there was no way anybody but us could possibly find the field. Dodger appeared next to Lizzie with a huge grin. He was fully decked out in a baseball uniform. Across the chest, it said CHIMPAGO CUBS. Next to him, in a neat pile, were two extra jerseys, a pair of mitts, and two sets of cleats. I held up one of the jerseys: It said NEW YORK MONKEES in fancy lettering. Dodger tossed the other one to Lizzie and shouted, "PLAY BALL!"

While Lizzie was pulling her jersey on over her school clothes, I grabbed Dodger's elbow and dragged him around the edge of the backstop. "What are you doing?" I hissed.

"Dude, you wanted me to solve your Lizzie problem, so that's what I'm doing! Plus, we're practicing baseball together, so this is like splitting two coconuts with one stone."

"Uh, the saying is 'killing two birds with one stone.'"

"Wow, you humans are, like, so violent."

"Oh yeah?" I pushed my hair back from my forehead so my bruise would show. "If humans are the violent ones, who did *this* to me? And anyway, how do you figure *this* is going to solve my Lizzie problem?"

"Because, dude, after this, you'll be great friends with her!"

Did you ever feel like someone was listening to you but completely not hearing what you were trying to tell them? Anyway, when we emerged from behind the backstop, Lizzie was wearing her jersey, her cleats, and even her mitt. "Wow, everything fits me perfectly! Thanks, Mister Orangutan!"

You know, if anyone else called him an orangutan, Dodger would flip out, or launch into some long speech about why chimps are far superior to orangutans. But all he said to Lizzie was, "No problem. I'm a chimpanzee, though. You can recognize us by our handsome, prominent ears and lively sense of fun! My name is Dodger, and I'm a close personal friend of Willie's. He's told me all about you, so I thought you might want to come and help me with his top secret practice regimen."

I couldn't believe it. I was also amazed at how Lizzie wasn't getting all freaked out by any of this. I mean, signs popping up in the middle of the sidewalk, self-rolling blue carpet trails, a magical baseball field, a talking blue chimp—she was going with the flow all the way. For a horrifying second, the thought crossed my mind that Lizzie might be kind of—well—*cool*.

Then she picked up a baseball and said, "I'll be glad to, Mr. Dodger. Can you show me how to make a touchdown?"

But believe it or not, the first half of practice went well. Dodger took the bat and made us take turns playing the infield and catching throws back to the plate. Even though Lizzie hadn't really played before, our infield skills were pretty similar, because of course my coaches always plunked me in right field, as far from the ball as they could put me. Dodger hit maybe a hundred grounders, and Lizzie and I only booted maybe thirty of them. Truthfully, we even kind of laughed together when one of us missed a play—which was a totally different experience from getting made fun of all through my team's practices. Maybe because I wasn't as nervous about getting teased, I really think I started improving after a while.

Then Dodger stopped hitting balls, stood up straight, and said, "It's time to put my Top Secret Coordination Improvement Plan into action."

As I trotted in from my position between second and third base, I asked, "And that would be . . . ?"

"Here, bud," Dodger said. "Take this." He whipped off his eye patch and held it out to me. My first thought was *YUCK!* I could only imagine what kind of horrible wound might be behind that thing, not to mention what my mom would say about putting on a chimp's used eye patch. When I got closer to him, though, I noticed that the eye that he'd just uncovered looked totally normal. It was also blinking repeatedly. Dodger said, "Wow, it sure is bright out here!"

"Uh, Dodger? You can see out of that eye?" I asked as I gingerly took the patch from him.

"Oh, sure, when I have to."

"Then why would you wear the eye patch?"

"It's for my image, bud. Makes me look tough!" He leaned closer and whispered, "Plus, the lady chimps love it." He raised his voice again. "Now put that thing over one eye and get back out in the field. Once you learn to throw and catch with the patch on, you'll totally *rule* without it!"

This sounded crazy. "Dodger, what makes you think this will make me a better player?"

"Well, remember the fat guy from the Yankees who ate all the hot dogs? It worked for him. We used to play some ball out behind his orphanage when he was a kid, and he couldn't hit to save his life until he tried the patch trick."

Whoa. If it was good enough for the Babe, it was good enough for me.

I hustled back into the field and slipped the patch on between my left eye and my glasses. It felt very weird, and I totally missed the first five or six grounders that Dodger hit to me. After that, I got better—not great, but better. Lizzie even got all excited to try the patch. Dodger said, "Wait, let's try some pop-ups first."

And that's how I wound up with a bloody nose.

Fortunately, the magical ball field came with a first-aid kit. Dodger stuffed a twisty cotton thing up each of my nostrils, then busted out with an ice pack, which he made me hold against one side of my rapidly swelling nose. As Dodger started raking the infield (he said we still had a couple more days to practice before my big game), Lizzie and I walked home on the blue carpet, which had reappeared right when we needed it. She said, "Well, that was a lot of fun. I mean, until the end part, obviously."

Through my blood-caked cotton nose plugs, I replied, "Yeh, id was."

She ignored my little speech problem and said, "I can't wait to do it again! Not necessarily the bleeding scene, but the rest of it. D'you think we could play again tomorrow? I could probably convince my mum that we needed to collect specimens for our terrariums. And, no offense, we still need to work on your ball-whacking."

"Ball-whacking?"

"You know, with the bat?" she clarified.

"Oh," I said. "Batting. It's called batting." She had a point. My team would hate me even more than they already did if I blew the last game and ruined our first-place finish. So it might be a good time for me to learn how to hit.

We reached the edge of my backyard. Through our dining-room window, I could see my mom and Lizzie's sitting at the table drinking coffee, with their heads bent over a big chart that said PLANNED SAFETY IMPROVEMENTS across the top. I could read the top three:

1. *Pad the playground: No ouchies!*
2. *Shatterproof lunch trays!*
3. *Buy helmets for dodgeball!*

Jeepers! Every kid in school knew my mom was the safety nut. If we all had to wear helmets for stupid dodgeball and run around on padding for recess every day, that would really help my popularity—*not!*

Anyway, Lizzie put a hand out and stopped me from walking into the moms' line of sight. "Hold on," she said. "Your mum will go absolutely mental if you walk in there with these bloody cotton thingies hanging out of your nose."

Again, Lizzie had a point. But I was afraid to pull the plugs out. I reached up and gently wiggled one experimentally. The slightest pressure made it feel as though an angry weasel were clawing its way up my nose into my brain.

Lizzie sighed, reached into her school backpack, and pulled out a wad of tissues. "Here, let me," she said.

"Uh, are you sure? It's going to be really gross." Plus, what if she made it hurt even more? And then what if I passed out in front of her? She would scream. My mom would freak and dial 911. I would wake up in a jet-powered helicopter, racing to the nearest hospital with a trauma center, and—

Lizzie sighed. "Honestly, Willie, it's no big

deal. I already know boys are gross." She grinned reassuringly, wrapped a couple of tissues around her thumb and first finger, and slowly reached up to pinch the end of one cotton thing. With great care, she eased it out of my nose. When it was in the clear, she let out a long breath. "See," she said, "no problem." She dropped the bloody cotton and tissues on the ground, got new tissues, and repeated the whole process with my other nostril. Then she said, "Okay, sir, it looks as though, with proper nursing care, you should pull through."

"Thank you," I said weakly.

"Don't mention it. By the way," Lizzie said, "I like your friend Dodger. I can't believe you have a real imaginary friend! I mean, a real friend who's imaginary. I mean, a—well, a blue chimp with powers! This is so cool! How did it happen?"

"Well, it's kind of a secret. I mean, I don't know if Dodger would want me to tell."

"Come on, Willie. Didn't he already show himself to me?"

I wasn't sure what I should do. And how did I know I could trust Lizzie? I knew Dodger thought she was special, but that didn't mean—

"Will, you can trust me. Dodger can be our own private secret! And I can keep a secret. That's what friends are for, isn't it?"

Just then, the moms looked up and saw us, so I was saved from answering. Lizzie picked up the bloody little pile from the lawn and we started walking across the yard. When we got to the back porch, where my dad keeps the garbage cans, she slipped the whole thing behind her back into one of the cans without even breaking stride. I had to admit, it was a slick move.

Man, my life was getting weird.

CHAPTER SEVEN

Grounded

I ALMOST GOT THROUGH the living room without my mom noticing my nose situation. I mean, she looked at me and Lizzie when we came inside to say hello, but she was figuring out some kind of big PTA budgeting problem on the calculator, so I don't think anything registered right away. Unfortunately, Amy was lying on the couch doing her homework, and she noticed instantly as I tried to glide toward the stairs without attracting too much close attention. "Oh, Willie!" Amy shrieked. "What happened to your nose? It's horrible!"

That got Mom's attention. She jumped up,

grabbed me by both arms, and said, "Are you all right? Oh, my buddy!" I could have died of humil-iation right there on the spot.

I mumbled, "I'm fine, Mom. It's just a—"

Before I could finish, Mom pulled my head to her chest in a bone-crushing hug. I caught a mo-mentary glimpse of Amy smirking with mischie-vous satisfaction, and then the flood came. A thick gout of blood splashed onto the white sweater Mom was wearing. She pushed me to arm's length and then started yelling. She yelled while Lizzie tried to explain that we had just been playing catch; Lizzie looked down at the floor and bit her bottom lip. Mom yelled some more while she dragged me to the bathroom and stuffed twisted tissues up my nose. She yelled while she dragged me down to the laundry room and poured stain re-mover all over the front of the sweater. She stopped yelling long enough to tell Lizzie, "William has to be careful when he plays—he's very delicate!" I could have sworn I saw Lizzie rolling her eyes at that one as Mom turned back to me and asked, "Why weren't you wearing your batting helmet?" I said, "Mom, people don't wear batting helmets to play catch." She fired back, "They do if they plan to use their face as a mitt!" On that embarrassing note, Lizzie and her mother left. Lizzie gave me a little look of sympathy as she stepped out the door, like you would give to your puppy as you were dropping it off in the kennel. But at the same time, I had this feeling she was trying not to laugh. Then Lizzie was gone, and Mom yelled some more. She told me that, since I kept getting hurt whenever I tried to go anywhere, I was grounded until I "earned back her trust." I tried pointing out to her that I had actually injured my forehead while closed up in the safety of my own room, but it didn't matter.

When your mom is as ridiculously overprotective as mine, nothing you say matters.

My nose was throbbing. I always hated to let my mom know I was in pain, because I didn't want her to decide I needed emergency surgery every time I had a hangnail, but I gave in this time and asked her for some aspirin. She told me that aspirin thins the blood, so she couldn't give it to me while I was bleeding. So I staggered upstairs to my room with a gigantic handful of tissues and a baggie full of ice cubes, and lay down on my bed. Staring over the ice bag at the ceiling, I thought about my confusing day. I had really been having fun with Dodger and Lizzie. Also, it was a relief that someone else had seen Dodger, because truthfully, I had been a tiny bit worried that I was going crazy. Even though I couldn't believe I was thinking it, I wanted to play with the two of them again.

It figured: for the month after Tim left, when I had zero friends and zero to do, I had been in no trouble at all. Now that I might have things to do and people (well, a girl and a blue chimp, but still) to do them with, I was probably going to be grounded until I died of old age.

Suddenly Dodger was sitting in the swivel chair at my desk. He swung to face me. "So, Willie, I think our first practice went pretty well. That Lizzie has some real potential."

I forgot all about my troubles for a second, glad to be talking baseball. "As what? A second baseman? A catcher? What do you think?"

Dodger snorted. "Dude, as a buddy for us! She's funny, and she has a cool accent. And she isn't all girly about blood."

Which, I had to admit, seemed to be a key quality if you were hanging out with Dodger.

"Plus, she sticks up for you. AND she passed the Special Person Test with the garbage on the ground. Wow, am I glad Part One of the Three-Part Plan is, like, Mission Accomplished. Now we can concentrate on getting your mom to trust you more. You're pushing eleven years old, dude. It's time for you to cut loose from the old apron strings! Get your groove on! Find your freedom! Climb every mountain! Ford every stream! Roam the world in search of adventure!"

"Uh, Dodger, when we got home, my mom saw my nose. She kinda flipped out. I'm grounded. Now I can't even roam the *block* in search of adventure!"

Dodger laughed. "Excellent," he said.

"Dodger, did you hear what I said? I'm grounded. I can't leave the house. Look around you—do you see any mountains or streams in here? Or any freedom?"

He scanned my room. I noticed that his eye patch was back in place, and so was his usual uniform of surfer shorts. "Nope, bud, all I see is apron strings. Lots and lots of apron strings. But that's good. The tighter a string is, the easier it is to cut."

What was that, some kind of chimpanzee riddle? A wave of pain flowed through my nose, and I lost my train of thought before I could ask. In the meantime, Dodger looked at the closet and caught sight of this dry-erase easel board that I had used to teach Amy her alphabet when she was in kindergarten. He dragged it out, rummaged around in the little attached plastic case for a marker, uncapped one, and started lecturing me:

"Willie, what we need to do is find a way for you to face danger and prove to your mom that you can take care of yourself."

"Well, couldn't I just avoid danger? If I stay safe for a while, won't that show her I can . . . I don't know . . . be safe?"

"Too slow, dude. You've spent ten years being safe, and where has it gotten you? Other guys your age are out playing football with no helmets, helping their dads use Weedwackers and lawn mowers, burning stuff with magnifying glasses. And here you are, chillin' with a chimp. No, little man, it's definitely time for action.

"Anyway, as I was saying, I have brainstormed a list of excellent danger sources." He started writing as he listed them. "They are:

1. *Poison*
2. *Cliff*
3. *Explosion*
4. *Fire*
5. *Electrocution*

"Now, the trick is, we need to come up with a way you can prove you're careful and trustworthy while doing something dangerous. So I think we can rule out POISON, because I can't think of anything good you can do with it. Same goes for . . . let's see . . . CLIFF . . . and EXPLOSION . . . ooh, and ELECTROCUTION is never any good. So the only one left is your answer: FIRE. We are going to win your mom over by harnessing the terrible power of FIRE!"

Jeepers, this sounded promising. Why hadn't I thought of impressing my mother with a nice bonfire? Or perhaps a lovely volcano in our backyard? Why didn't I just handcuff myself to my bed, throw away the key, and save my mom the trouble of grounding me for life? "Dodger?" I asked. "Couldn't I just wish for my mom to trust me? And you could, like, make it happen?"

Dodger frowned and said, "Dude, *you've* got to trust *me*. Just think: You've only known me for, like, two days, and I've already solved a third of your life's problems. So let's do this my way. I ask you, what could possibly go wrong?"

Ha.

Before I could even begin to list the many, many things that could go wrong when one combined the concept of Dodger with the concept of fire, my bedroom door swung open. My mom stepped in, took one look at the dry-erase board, and started screaming.

The next day at school, I tried to explain the whole ugly scene to Lizzie, who refused to stop laughing. She especially loved the part where my mom saw Dodger's list of excellent danger sources and went completely bonkers. I kept saying, "What's so funny?" and, "I'm serious!" None of that had any effect at all, though. Lizzie would just get quiet for a brief moment and then start in again, like, "The thing your mum said about using your face as a mitt—that was completely brilliant! My mum and I laughed for about three blocks. I mean, not about your nose getting smashed or anything, just about your mum's reaction. So, are you up for some baseball training after school, then? You still need to practice thumping the ball with the bat before the weekend."

I don't know which part of "I'm grounded" she didn't understand.

When I got home, my mom and sister were out at their weekly mother-daughter Brownies meeting. My dad was home, though, working like he always does in his basement office. He ordered me to go right to my room and do all of my homework before my mom got home at five o'clock. As he put it, "Please get your work done—and don't break anything. Mom will kill us both if you get in any more trouble this week." So, being the good boy that I am, I went straight to my room and did my homework. After a while I got tired of this really boring fractions worksheet I was doing and started daydreaming about how great life could be if Dodger gave me three wishes. I pictured myself driving my very own sports car up the driveway of my mansion, headed for my private video arcade for a few quick days of gaming on the way to Yankee Stadium for my major league debut. The radio was tuned to a sports station, and the announcers were discussing my amazing abilities:

Well, Jon, it's a beautiful day at the stadium today, a perfect day for the youngest shortstop in big-league history to begin his Hall of Fame career.

Yes, Susan, this should be one to remember. Willie Ryan has already earned the awed respect of a nation with his incredible two-week climb through the minor leagues. It's hard to believe that just two Tuesdays ago, this kid was a batboy for a single-A farm team.

You know, Jon, it really is hard to believe. Baseball historians will be talking about this for decades, trying to understand it. Me, I'm just trying to pick out my favorite Willie Ryan moment so far. Was it the three home runs he hit in that last game in Philadelphia?

Maybe, but that wasn't much of a challenge for him, since he only had his eyes closed when he hit those. I kind of liked the wild pitch when he stole first, second, third, and home before the catcher even had time to pick up the ball.

I have to admit, that wasn't bad. But what about the time when he was playing left field and jumped twenty feet straight up to spear that line drive—without a mitt?

Yes, folks, it's been an amazing half-month since fifth grade let out for summer vacation. And now a nation awaits this game. A gasp goes up from the crowd: Willie's personal batboy, Derek Jeter, has just come onto the field carrying the young star's equipment. The question on everyone's lips is this: If things go well today, do you think Willie Ryan's mom might let him take off that stupid helmet?

I rubbed my eyes and tried to get back to my worksheet. But I couldn't stop thinking. I had to plan my wishes just right if I was going to fix everything and give myself a perfect life.

Suddenly, I heard a *POOF!* This was followed by some gruesome munching noises. I turned toward my bed and was startled to see Dodger sitting there with his whole forearm in a white bag. There was powdered sugar all around his mouth, and when he pulled his hand out of the bag I found out why: He was holding a fistful of doughnut holes.

I love doughnut holes. He held out the bag to me and said, "Want some? Go ahead. Just reach in and wish for doughnut holes."

Trying hard not to think of all the fur that was probably stuck to the inner walls of the bag, I reached in and felt around. The bag was empty. "Ha-ha, very funny," I said. "You know, I don't go around tricking *you*."

Dodger's eyes widened. "What are you talking about, dude? Give me that bag!" I did, and he shoved his hand in again. It came out holding a chocolate-covered banana. He winked at me and ate the entire thing in two huge gulps. Well, he didn't exactly eat the whole thing; about half of the chocolate ended up smeared on his face. "The food is there for you, buddy," he said. "You've just gotta want it."

I grabbed the bag back from him and reached in again. It was empty! I said, "I wish this stupid bag was full of chocolate doughnut holes!" I felt the bag expand in my hand, peeked in, and saw a nice pile of steaming-fresh doughnut holes. Now this was more like it! Dodger watched with amusement as I shoved about nine of those babies in my mouth at once. I nearly choked, but they were so good, I just couldn't stop myself. These were the best doughnut holes I had ever tasted! They were perfect! I could eat them forever and not get tired of them.

I grabbed handful after handful, popping them in my mouth at top speed. For about a minute, I was totally satisfied. Then I started thinking, *Wouldn't the doughnut holes be better with milk? I wish there were some milk in the bag.* With a strange slurping noise, the bag started getting heavier and heavier. I looked in and saw that the doughnut holes were now floating in a rapidly rising sea of milk. Oh, man—that wish hadn't quite come out right. I looked over at Dodger, who was smirking at me.

"What do I do now? The milk is going to overflow!"

Dodger said, "What milk?"

I said, "Well, the doughnut holes got kind of dry after a while, so I wished for some milk."

Dodger started cleaning his nails with one of my homework pens. I didn't have time to think about how gross that was, though, because the milk was starting to spill over the edge of the bag onto the hardwood floor. It was clear that Dodger wasn't about to jump to my rescue, so this was up to me. I said, "I wish the bag were bigger!"

The bag seemed to swell in my hands, and for a moment, the milk stopped spilling over the top. Then it overflowed again. I said, "I wish the bag were sealed at the top!" Instantly the bag had a domed top. The milk was contained! But the bag kept getting heavier and heavier. I could barely even hold it. And the milk was still expanding inside.

I looked at Dodger and said, "Do something!"

He said, "I did. I gave you my awesome doughnut bag."

"But—" I said. "But—it's going to explode!"

"You wanted to make wishes, dude. Maybe you should start wishing for a raincoat."

"A raincoat?" I asked shakily. The bag was getting so heavy that I could barely speak.

"Yeah," he said, "for when it—"

He didn't get a chance to finish his sentence because just then, the bag popped. I shook my head to get the gooky mixture of milk and chocolate doughnut bits out of my eyes, and looked around in horror. Every surface of the entire room was coated in milk, chocolate, and shreds of paper.

"My room!" I shouted.

"Dude, my doughnut bag!" Dodger replied.

We glared at each other. Then I thought of something: My mom would be home by five. I looked at my wall clock, but couldn't see the hands through the mess. I wiped the face with my sleeve and saw that it was 4:30. I only had half an hour!

"Bet you wish you could get this cleaned up in thirty minutes, huh?" Dodger said.

Oh, jeepers! "*Yes*, I wish I could get this cleaned up in thirty minutes!"

Dodger winked at me and loped out of the room, heading down the hall toward our bathroom. He was gone for maybe a minute, while I debated running away from home before my mom saw the mess I had made because of Dodger. Then he came back balancing a bucket, a mop, and my mom's big box of cleaning supplies. He handed me the mop and said, "Your wish just came true, buddy. You can get this cleaned up in thirty minutes."

"But that's not what I meant! I meant, like, you should make the mess go *POOF*!"

Dodger settled himself back on my bed, which had miraculously been missed by all of the flying goop. As he began picking his toes, he sighed contentedly. Then he said, "Dude, I'm tired. Wishes are *never* as fun as you think they're gonna be!"

I pulled on my mom's hot-pink rubber gloves, and Dodger started humming to himself. The tune sounded a lot like "Take Me Out to the Ball Game."

CHAPTER EIGHT

Of Fish and Fire

WHEN MY MOM GOT HOME that night, I had cleaned up every square inch of my room. The walls were shiny, the floor was sparkling, and every flat surface was dust-free. The place had a strange odor of chocolate, milk, and lemony freshness, but thankfully, Mom just focused on the cleanliness. She took one look around, sniffed the air, and said, "Good job cleaning your room, William. Is your homework all done? If it is, I might even consider ungrounding you for your baseball game this weekend. Do you think you can avoid destroying anything until then?"

I nodded. Meanwhile, behind her, Dodger was

picking little specks of chocolate out of his chest fur and eating them. He looked up at me and winked, then snapped his fingers and disappeared. I had a feeling that avoiding destruction would be harder than she thought.

In the morning, Mom told me that she had a meeting after school, so I should stay at the school after-care room until she picked me up at 5:30. But at lunch, Lizzie told me that I had to sneak out before after-care and go home right at three. She wouldn't tell me why. I explained the grounding situation yet AGAIN, and even told her that if I got busted for anything before Saturday, my mom wouldn't let me play my last ball game. I *had* to play that game. The whole team would think I was a total chicken-weasel if I missed it.

Plus, I never sneak out of anything. I'm not a "breaks the rules" kind of kid—I'm a "terrified of breaking Mom's rules" kind of kid. I guess I just take after my dad.

But Lizzie didn't back down. She insisted that she had a plan for getting me more freedom for years to come. I said that she should just go ahead and work on her plan alone if it was so important.

Then she replied with the scariest eleven words in the English language: "I won't be alone. I'll be with Dodger—in your house!"

So that's why I was pacing back and forth in the front hallway of my house at ten after three, peeking through the curtains every few seconds for signs of my insane new buddies. I felt like a criminal, and I was about ninety-five percent sure I was going to get busted, big-time. I was also really thirsty after sprinting the ten blocks from school to my house, so I tore myself away from the windows for a moment to get a drink of water from the kitchen. That's when the doorbell rang.

When I opened the door, I could have screamed. Standing there with loaded shopping bags in their hands were Dodger and Lizzie. They stepped inside, smiling dementedly at me. I slammed the door behind them as quickly as possible.

"Uh, guys? What in the world are you doing here? What's this plan of yours? I am so dead. If my mom and dad go to pick me up at after-care and I'm not there, I'm dead."

"Chill. You'll be back at the after-care room in plenty of time for your mom. Trust me!"

"And if my mom and dad come home and find Lizzie, I'm dead. I'm supposed to be grounded."

"Right," Dodger said. "That's why we're not taking you anywhere except back to the school. Duh!"

"But 'grounded' also means 'no friends over.' "

"Nah, that's 'unfriended.' It's much more serious than 'grounded.' And you're not in nearly enough trouble to be unfriended. Believe me."

While Dodger did his usual alarming job of trying to be logical, Lizzie stomped into the kitchen and dropped her bags on the counter. I gave up on arguing with Dodger and followed her. She started unpacking. First she pulled out a bunch of bananas and placed it on the countertop. Then she placed a paper-wrapped bundle that said SEAFOOD next to the bananas. Reaching back into the bag, she removed another bunch of bananas, followed by a six-pack of banana yogurt shakes, a clove of garlic, an onion, a box of banana wafer cookies, a bag of tossed salad, several jars of banana baby food, two boxes of spaghetti, a can of crushed tomatoes, more bananas, a little plastic container of Italian herb mix, a copy of *National Geographic*, and a five-pound bag of sugar.

Dodger put his bags next to Lizzie's and piled up several more banana products on the counter. Then he panicked, dashed all around the room, poked his head into each of his now-empty bags, and reached into Lizzie's bag, which was still on the counter. With a look of relief, he gently pulled out a bunch of grapes and popped a grape in his mouth. "Wow, I thought we had left these back at the market!" he said.

"Dodger, what are you doing with all these groceries?" I asked.

"Unpacking."

"I know *that*. I mean, why are you unpacking them all over our kitchen?"

"Dude, the kitchen is where groceries go."

"No, I mean . . ." I stopped for a second and rubbed my eyes. I could feel a headache coming on. "What are we supposed to do with the groceries?"

Dodger beamed at me. "Tonight," he exclaimed, "you conquer fire!"

Oh, no. Oh, no, no, *no*. "Con . . . conquer . . . fire?" I stuttered.

Lizzie interjected. "Yes, Willie. Dodger explained all of your problems while we were at the store—how you're a total failure at baseball, how your mum won't trust you to do anything without injuring yourself, and how you were too shy to be friends with me. So we're fixing the mum part by making a delicious dinner for your family. We're conquering fire by *cooking*, get it? When your mum sees how excellent you are at handling the responsibility of cooking a meal for your family, I'm quite sure she will unground you. And then we can work more on doing baseball. We still have two more days to practice before your last game!"

She started showing me various items on the counter and explaining how we could use them to make our meal. Apparently, if we chopped up the onion and garlic, fried them up in oil for a few minutes, and then dumped in the can of crushed tomatoes and some of the Italian herb mix, we'd get spaghetti sauce. If we boiled a pot of water and threw in the spaghetti, we'd get cooked spaghetti. If we dumped the bag of salad into a big bowl, we'd have—well—a salad. And the seafood was to make—

"Hey, Lizzie," I asked. "What's the seafood for, again?"

"You'll see."

"And how about the banana stuff?"

Dodger said, "What, doesn't the chimp deserve a little treat now and then? Oh, sure, the people get the fish, the salad, the spaghetti. And the chimp is just supposed to sit there and suffer? Sheesh."

"Oh," I said. My headache was coming on a lot faster now. "Sorry, Dodger. I know how much you like bananas. And the grapes?"

"They're for variety. What am I supposed to do, eat nothing but bananas?"

"And, um, the *National Geographic*?"

"Well, I like the pictures. Besides, I know some of the models. My uncle Joe was on the cover once."

All right, then. It was time to cook. If we were going to burn down my house, we might as well get started. Otherwise, my family might get home before we were finished with the job. Lizzie and I started rummaging around the kitchen for cooking utensils. Dodger reclined on the floor, put both feet up on my seat at the table, and fed himself grapes.

Within minutes, we had a bizarre assortment of plates, pots, pans, cutting boards, and assorted gadgets spread across every available surface. I was totally clueless about this stuff, mostly because my mom generally didn't let me handle anything sharper than a spoon. But Lizzie seemed to know what she was doing, and soon she was chopping vegetables, barking orders at me, making Dodger fill pots with water, and yelling at both of us just because Dodger was shedding his fur all over the side dishes.

I had never realized how hectic cooking could be.

After twenty minutes or so, the kitchen started to smell good. The salad was in a fancy bowl, all ready to go. The onions and garlic were slowly cooking in a pot, while the spaghetti water heated on the next burner. "And now," pronounced Lizzie, "it is time for the main course!" She held up the bundle of seafood.

"Okay, now will you tell me what's in there?" I asked.

"Well, it's salmon. I got it to make your mum's favorite dish."

This was puzzling. I had been living with my mom for more than ten years, and she had never eaten salmon in my presence. Lizzie continued, "See, your mum and my mum were chatting at our kitchen table one day when they were working on this PTA report, and your mum was telling mine about her favorite food: sweetish fish. I don't think we have that in England. I asked the man at the store for the sweetest fish they had, and he said they didn't have sweet fish, but that this one kind would taste good with a sweet sauce. So here we are." She grinned. "Oh, your mum will be so delighted!"

Sweetish fish? Sweetish fish? My mom's favorite food was—OH, JEEPERS! "Lizzie, Dodger, I hate to break this to you, but my mom's favorite food isn't fish at all. It's candy!"

Lizzie looked disgusted. "Fish-flavored candy? What kind of crazy treat is fish-flavored candy? No offense, but holy mackerel—that is really gross!"

"No, you still don't get it. Her favorite food is Swedish fish. S-W-E-D-I-S-H fish. They're these red, sort of transparent goo candies."

"Oh, they're *goo candies*," Dodger chimed in. "That sounds much better!"

"Listen, Dodger, it doesn't matter whether you think Swedish fish sounds like a delightful snack. What matters is that now we have this stinky salmon and a bag of sugar. How are we supposed to turn salmon and sugar into a main course?"

While Dodger and I continued to argue, Lizzie marched over to the counter, ripped the wrapping off the fish, and slapped the filets onto a cookie sheet. Then she stabbed a hole in the top of the sugar bag with a knife and poured the sugar all over each piece of fish. "Don't worry," she said. "Sugar tastes good, right? And the fish man said salmon would taste good with a sweet sauce. So this should be fine. It will be our invention. We can call it Sweet Salmon Surprise! What do you think, Willie?"

I thought it would definitely be a surprise. I just didn't realize quite how big the surprise would be. Lizzie put the salmon in the oven and

107

told me and Dodger to set the table. We went into the dining room, turned on the lights, and started going back and forth to the kitchen with spoons, forks, napkins, and knives. Then Dodger shouted, "Dude! Heads up!" and started tossing the little wooden salad bowls to me one by one. Apparently, he felt that we could practice my baseball skills while we worked. Needless to say, I didn't think this was a great plan.

"Wait," I said. "I'm not ready!"

"Oh, come on, bud," he replied, flipping another bowl in my direction. "Setting the table is boring. Let's have some fun!"

As I caught the second bowl, I said, "I'm serious, Dodger. We're going to break something!"

He just giggled and kept the bowls flying. Actually, I didn't do too badly with them—I only dropped one of the four we'd need for my family. I made sure that the bowl hadn't cracked on impact with the floor and breathed a little sigh of relief. But the sigh turned into a gasp when I realized that Dodger wasn't stopping with the bowls. By the time I could say anything, one of my mom's best china dinner plates was hurtling toward me like the world's most expensive Frisbee. I gasped, "No, not the china!"

Dodger giggled some more. I managed to catch the plate—barely—and just got it onto the table in time to whip back around and try to grab the next one.

The key word there was *try*. The plate flew right between my outstretched palms and shattered all over the floor beneath my father's chair. Dodger shrugged as he ambled over to me. "Oops, my bad," he said. "But hey, it's no big deal. They probably won't be throwing plates your way at the big game."

As I knelt and started picking up the largest fragments of the broken plate, I shouted at him, "Gee, you're probably right, Mr. Banana-Munching Super-Genius. Thanks for making that excellent point!"

Even though he was completely wrong in this situation, Dodger yelled right back at me, "Oh, sure, make with the chimp jokes. Dude, I build you your own personal stadium, recruit Lizzie to be your friend, and take her food shopping WITH MY OWN MONEY so we can get YOUR mom to stop treating you like a five-year-old. We're having a great time, making some quality food, and now you get all personal just because YOU drop one measly—"

"You're blaming me for dropping the plate? How do you know it's my fault? Did it ever occur to you that maybe it might be hard to catch something that's hurled at you BY A CHIMP WITH AN EYE PATCH?"

"You ungrateful—"

"You crazy—"

We were both stopped in the middle of our insults when Lizzie stepped through the doorway and said, "Uh, guys?" I turned to her and put my hands to my head. Behind her, a thick cloud of black smoke was rolling right at us. She said, "I don't know what happened. I put the salmon in and turned the oven to five hundred degrees so it would cook nice and fast, and now—"

Dodger and I both ran past Lizzie into the kitchen. The room was filling up quickly with smoke. It also smelled horrible, like some unholy mix of fish guts and cotton candy. Apparently, Sweet Salmon Surprise and high heat was a bad combination. I opened the oven door, which re-leased even more smoke. Then Dodger shoved some oven mitts on his hands, reached in, and grabbed the cookie sheet that had the flaming fish on it. He staggered over to the sink and flooded the whole thing with water. Steam mixed with the smoke, and Dodger stepped back. The fire was out, which was a good thing. However, the whole house was filled with terrible, oily fish-smoke, which was not so good. I looked at the clock. It was 5:07—also not so good. How was I going to salvage the dinner, get the house cleaned up, and somehow sneak back to the school in time to get picked up in only twenty-three minutes?

Lizzie gasped, "I'm sorry, Willie."

I said, "Oh, man, I am in trouble."

Dodger said, "You're not in trouble. See, I'm opening the window. Now we'll just whip the pasta into shape, and then spray some air freshener around."

Lizzie said, "Umm, Dodger? Willie?" She pointed to the stove, where the spaghetti pot was boiling over frantically. The starchy water was bubbling and hissing as it ran down into the burner.

Dodger said, "You're still okay, dude. We'll just—"

At that precise moment, I heard the front door of the house burst open and smash against the wall, followed by my mom's voice: "WILLIAM BENNETT RYAN!"

I froze, paralyzed with terror. Lizzie turned about three shades of whitish green. We both looked at Dodger, who shook his head and said, "Oh, dude. *Now* you're in trouble!"

CHAPTER NINE

Bottled Hope, Incorporated

I LOOKED AT LIZZIE. Lizzie looked at me. I looked at Dodger. Dodger turned on his heels and ran out of the room. I knew that in about four seconds my mom was going to come pounding into the room and throw the kind of fit you don't usually get to see unless you're watching *When Bears Attack*. Lizzie stumbled over to the stove and turned off the burner under the spaghetti. I tried hard not to whimper or flee.

I could hear my mom barreling down the hallway, yelling. I had three seconds to live . . . two . . . one . . .

POOF!

Just then, some guy in puffy pants, a vest, and a turban appeared right in front of me. He snapped his fingers, and everything got silent— dead silent. The hissing of the spaghetti water on the burner stopped. My mom's shrieking ceased. I couldn't even hear any street sounds through the open window. I noticed that nothing was moving; even the wisps of smoke in the air were just hanging there. Lizzie said to me, "Hey, what's happening? Who's this guy?"

Great. This was my idea of a perfect world—my house filled with smoke, my mom about to wring my neck, Dodger in hiding, and everyone on the planet frozen in place except for me and Lizzie. "Uh, I have no idea." Trying hard not to scream, cry, or burst into hysterical laughter, I forced myself to say, "Excuse me, sir. Would you mind telling me who you are and what's going on?"

He gave me a snooty look and said, "I, sir, am the Great Lasorda, Genie, First Class, president of Bottled Hope, Incorporated. *Surely* my little helper has told you all about me."

"Little helper?"

"You know, my pet chimpanzee, Dodger."

"Pet chimpanzee? *Pet* chimpanzee? You mean Dodger isn't a genie?"

The Great Lasorda snorted at me. "Dodger, a genie? Please, be serious. I mean, I know there's a tremendous magical-labor shortage, but what in the world gave you the idea that *Dodger* was a genie?"

"Well, he lives in a lamp, and he has powers and all, plus I'm pretty sure he said—"

The Great Lasorda was beginning to turn a scary shade of red. His voice sounded too calm, the way my school's principal sounds right before he goes ballistic in the lunchroom. "You think Dodger has powers? Why? All right, let me guess. He showed you the Field of Dreams?"

That must have been the blue baseball diamond. I nodded.

"And the Bottomless Well of Treats?"

Ooh, the doughnut bag that had blown up all over my room. I nodded again.

"And the *POOF!* trick? Disappearing and all that? And reading your mind a bit?"

I nodded twice.

"Oh, and I suppose he probably took you for a little ride on the Magic Carpet of Khartoum?"

I shook my head. What the heck was a Magic Carpet of Khartoum?

"So, William Bennett Ryan, let me get this straight. All Dodger did was show you a few little parlor tricks, and you thought he was . . . a *genie*?"

"Well, he kind of—"

Now the Great Lasorda's face was starting to look as purple as his vest. "He kind of what? Did Dodger intentionally lead you to believe that he was a genie? Because if he did, he will be punished severely. I don't know why I should be surprised. After all, it's not like this would be the first time." He snapped his fingers, and Dodger appeared, looking almost scared.

The Great Lasorda said, "Dodger, have you explained to young William what your name stands for?"

Dodger gulped. "No, sir."

"And have you explained your exact job description in accordance with the by-laws of Bottled

Hope, Incorporated, Section Seven, Paragraph Five-B?"

Dodger turned away, and I could have sworn I heard a catch in his voice. "No, sir."

The Great Lasorda sighed, rolled his eyes to the ceiling, and said, "William, Dodger should have explained to you that his name is an acronym. It stands for Deputy On-call Dispatch Genie, Emergency Reserve (Third Class)."

"Wait, so he is a genie, then?" I wanted Dodger to be a genie—*my* genie. "It says *genie* in his name."

The Great Lasorda snapped, "Dodger is NOT a genie. He is a DEPUTY, EMERGENCY RE-SERVE genie (third class)."

"Then why did he come out when I rubbed the, uh, disguised teapot-thing? If you're the genie, shouldn't you have been the one who popped out?"

Dodger snorted. Now he looked more angry than scared. "Yeah," he said, "except the Great Lasorda was too busy to answer a plain old dispatch call. What was the emergency this time, O Mighty One? Did you need to spend two months at the Crystal Springs of Shalla-Bal again, making sure the temperature was just right? Or maybe you were taking your yearly urgent trip to the Sahara Palms Sandstorm Spa to make sure the sunbathing dunes are still in tip-top shape?"

Dodger looked at me. "Dude, this guy once spent forty years making a bunch of Israelites wander around the desert, just so he could get a deep tan."

The Great Lasorda snarled, "ENOUGH! When you found the lamp, I was otherwise occupied, and there was no other genie available. In fact, there was no deputy genie available. There was no deputy, emergency genie available. And THAT is why you got a deputy, emergency reserve genie (third class)." He took a deep breath, and when he spoke again, his voice had a dangerously false sweetness. "A deputy, emergency reserve genie (third class) who concealed his true job description and mission from the client."

"Client?" I asked.

"That would be you," Dodger muttered.

"And his true job description? What do you mean, his true job description?"

Dodger was looking down at his feet as the

Great Lasorda responded. "Generally, deputy, emergency reserve genies (third class) are dispatched to people who fit a certain, *ahem*, profile. They serve as companion animals to children who . . ."

Companion animals? Jeepers.

". . . have special friendship needs. Just as seeing eye dogs help those who have visual challenges, and police dogs use their sharp sense of smell to make up for their masters' dull noses, Dodger is here to make up for your . . . friendship impairment."

I couldn't believe this! "Friendship impairment? So Dodger appeared because I'm a—a—a *loser*?"

The Great Lasorda gave me an oily smile. "Please, William, *loser* is such an ugly word. We prefer to think of our clients as 'victory-challenged.' "

"Wait a minute, Mr. . . . uh . . . the Great. I am *not* a loser!"

The Great Lasorda cleared his throat and raised his eyebrows.

"Okay, I mean, I am *not* victory-challenged. Look, I have two friends right here: Dodger and Lizzie."

"Ah," said the Great Lasorda, "but Dodger is here because it is his job. And Lizzie . . . Lizzie, Lizzie, Lizzie. Why don't you tell Mr. Ryan why you have been following him around for the past month?"

Through this whole conversation, Lizzie had been so quiet that I had nearly forgotten she was there. But at the Great Lasorda's words, she blushed and started stammering. "Well, Willie, I'm here because I'm your . . . friend. Right? We're . . . we're buddies, aren't we?" She looked at the Great Lasorda with a hopeful little half-smile, the way I smile at Amy when I don't want her to say something that will get me in trouble.

The Great Lasorda raised his eyebrows again. "And would you please tell William exactly why you have pursued a friendship with him?"

What the heck was this guy talking about? Lizzie had always been around. And when Tim left town, she had just—

"Um, Willie?" Lizzie said, not quite looking in my eyes. "I started hanging around you this month because—because I made a promise."

"A promise? What are you talking about, Lizzie? You never promised me anything."

Now her eyes did meet mine for a split second. "I didn't promise *you*, Willie. I promised Tim that I would watch out for you. He was . . ." She paused and looked to the Great Lasorda, who nodded at her. "He was worried that you wouldn't have any friends after he left."

I couldn't believe it. The whole time Lizzie had been hanging around me, I'd flattered myself into thinking she was desperate to be my friend. And really, the entire time, I had been the desperate one. Jeepers, I *was* victory-challenged. Severely.

I just wished I could crawl into Dodger's bottle and hide for about a thousand years.

The Great Lasorda said, "As you can see, William, Dodger's intervention has been a complete failure. If I am not mistaken—and I am *never* mistaken—there were three wishes in your heart, as follows:

1. To make 'Dumb Old Lizzie from England' stop following you around;

2. To make your mother trust you with your own safety;

And 3. To turn you into a baseball star.

Have any of those goals been achieved?"

I looked at Lizzie, who was now glaring at me, and Dodger, who was giving me puppy-dog eyes (well, one puppy-dog eye, anyway). I didn't say anything. I didn't know what to say.

"Well? Lizzie has spent half of this week hanging around with you. Your mother is about to burst into this kitchen and ground you until you're old enough for her to start grounding your children. And all you have to show for your baseball practice is a swollen nose."

Dodger interjected, "Oh, sure, when you put it that way it all sounds bad. But what about all the fun we've been having? And, Willie, isn't it better having Lizzie as a friend?"

Lizzie snarled, "I am NOT that boy's friend!" Then she ran out of the kitchen and into the dining room, sobbing.

The Great Lasorda said, "Oh, yes, Dodger, I can see how your campaign to free Willie from his problems has been a flaming success so far. Right, Willie?"

I couldn't even look at him.

"And so," the Great Lasorda continued, "please accept my personal and professional apologies on behalf of Bottled Hope, Incorporated. In consideration of the disappointing service you have received from us so far"—he paused to glare at Dodger—"I hereby guarantee that you will receive full personal attention for the remainder of this week. You will be granted the standard Three Wishes Upgrade, of course. Will that be satisfactory, William?"

Wow, three wishes! I looked around at the smoky, messy kitchen, the spill-stained stove, the shattered bits of china I could see through the dining room doorway, and the long shadow of my mother reaching in from the hall. If I had ever needed three wishes, this was the time. The Great Lasorda was looking right at me, so he couldn't see that Dodger was shaking his head and making neck-cutting signals. I didn't see what the big deal was, though. How could getting three wishes possibly be a bad thing? I looked back and forth between Dodger and the genie, both of whom were waiting for my answer.

"Uh, sure," I said. "Three wishes sounds great!"

The Great Lasorda smiled. His smile was a little

sinister, but hey, I could live with a little creepiness if it got me out of this mess in one piece. "Excellent," he said. "Then I'll just banish our mischievous little chimp back to his lamp, and we can get to work on making your wishes come true."

"Wait a minute," I said. "Banish Dodger?"

Dodger blurted out, "Wait a minute, Your Greatness! I want to stay here. I want to help Willie!"

The Great Lasorda snorted. "I think I can handle three simple wishes on my own, thanks. It's bad enough I'll have to clean up for what you have already done, without having to monkey-sit you for several days as well. Now, all I need is for Willie to say the word, and you can go eat a nice banana in your little lamp. How about it, Willie? Are you ready to get everything you could ask for?"

The Great Lasorda smirked at me expectantly. Dodger was still making with the sad-puppy face, and I knew the "monkey" comment must have bothered him a lot. For a moment, I felt really sorry for him. We had definitely had some fun together, even if things hadn't worked out right. But then I looked around at the wreckage of my house. I thought about what was going to happen if my mom saw the smoking ruins of the kitchen. And, as a distant *SLAM!* let me know that Lizzie had made her way out the front door, I made up my mind. I needed a miracle. I needed three wishes. "I'm sorry, Dodger," I said.

Dodger looked totally crushed. His shoulders sagged, and he looked away from me at the wall. He muttered, "So am I, dude. I was your frie—" Just then, the Great Lasorda snapped his fingers, and Dodger was gone. All that was left was a chimp-shaped hole in the smoke.

CHAPTER TEN

Happily Ever After Dinner

SO THE GREAT LASORDA and I had a little talk, and he granted my first two wishes. From the moment he snapped his fingers again, Lizzie would bother me no more, and my mother would have full and complete trust in me. He asked, "Are you ready? Because once I grant these wishes of yours, things will be very, very different."

I took a deep breath, coughed out some smoke, and nodded. The Great Lasorda snapped his magic fingers. And *POOF*! The smoke disappeared. The mess on the stove disappeared. The Great Lasorda disappeared. The smashed china plate reassembled itself and flew onto the table, which was now miraculously set. The delicious, spicy aroma of well-cooked homemade food filled the kitchen, and I saw that several steaming pots were sitting on potholders on our breakfast bar with serving spoons sticking out of them. The Great Lasorda was pretty obnoxious, but apparently, he knew how to make things happen.

I braced myself for my mom's frightening entrance, but she came in smiling. My dad followed behind, listening intently as Amy rattled on about some girl who had fallen on the playground. My mom turned to her and said, "Oh, honey, it's too bad that your friend fell down. But these things happen. What do you expect the school to do, pad the whole school yard?" The whole family shared a big chuckle over that one, although I had to force my laugh out a second after everybody else's.

Then my dad said, "Hey, Will, you made dinner! Excellent! What is it?"

"Uh, it's a surprise," I stammered.

"Well, surprise us, then," my mom said as they trooped to the table and sat down. "I love surprises!"

Jeepers, my mom had always hated surprises.

I sat down, too, and said, "I wasn't sure who would want what, so I decided you can all just, uh, serve yourselves. Unless you think it's not safe for Amy to walk with hot food, I mean."

Mom and Dad looked at me funny, and Amy jumped up to serve herself. I said, "Hey, by the way, I'm sorry I left school before after-care. I had this, um, emergency project to do, plus I wanted to have time to cook this special meal for you."

Mom said, "After-care? When was the last time you went to after-care?"

Dad chimed in, "Yes, Will, you've been taking care of yourself after school for over a year now. Why would today be any different? Are you feeling all right? You're acting kind of, well, confused all of a sudden."

I took a sip of water. All of these changes were making me dizzy. Mom said, "Oh, James, he's fine. I wish you wouldn't baby him all the time!"

I tried not to choke on my water as Amy came back to the table with her plate heaped high. She had a steak knife teetering on the edge of her plate, and I had to resist the urge to tell her to be careful. Mom and Dad didn't even notice that their seven-year-old daughter had a razor-sharp object balanced mere inches above her lap.

For the first time, I got a good look at the food I had supposedly made. Apparently, I had whipped up a big old pot of chili, along with corn bread, rice, and a salad. I got myself some, and I had to admit, I'm a heck of an imaginary cook. Still, I couldn't get over how my whole family was acting like this was one hundred percent normal in our house. Just to make some conversation, I said, "So, Mom, how was the Safety Committee meeting?"

Now it was her turn to nearly gag on her drink. "Safety Committee meeting? How in the world would I know? I was down the hall at the Physical Education Advisory Board session. Good news, Will—they're finally going to put in that rock-climbing wall I've been pushing for!"

Wow, it was like my mom had been beamed into outer space and replaced by a supercool alien mom. But rock climbing terrifies me.

Mom continued, "You know, Will, this chili is SUPER!"

Amy nodded and grunted. Neither of my

parents even scolded her for trying to talk with her mouth full. My dad asked, "Did you have fun making this? It sure tastes like you put a lot of effort into it."

"Uh, yeah, Dad. It was quite an adventure."

"Well, you know what I always say, son: Every day should be an adventure!"

I smiled weakly at him, wondering whether he had *ever* said that before. I was pretty sure that if he had, my mom—the old mom—would have straightened him out pretty fast. "By the way," Dad continued, "I have a proposal for you. Seeing as how you enjoyed cooking so much, and we're all enjoying eating what you made, why don't we make this a routine? You could cook for us every Tuesday and Thursday, when your mother has her meetings."

I concentrated on forcing my face muscles into a weak little smile. "That sounds great, Dad."

Mom was beaming at me. "Oh, Will, we're so proud of you. You set a challenge for yourself and rose to the occasion. You're really turning into a responsible young man."

Jeepers. Nobody had blinked an eye about my

coming home and staying in the house alone after school. Nobody had even questioned where all of the food had come from, or how I had known what to do with it. And worst of all, they wanted me to do the whole thing again, twice a week. I wasn't sure how I'd pull that one off, especially since my three wishes would be used up long before next Tuesday. Plus, even though I'll deny this if anyone repeats it, the thought of being home alone scares me.

After dinner, when I went up to my room, the Great Lasorda was hovering in the air over my desk with his feet crossed over each other. I got the feeling he had been taking a nap, but his eyes opened when I came in. He said, "I trust that your dinner with the family went well?"

"I guess so," I said.

"Excellent! That's two wishes down, and one to go. With any luck I'll be free by . . . I mean, you will have everything you've always wanted by Saturday." He looked totally satisfied with himself as his eyes fluttered shut again.

I suddenly realized I wasn't tired at all—my head was buzzing with all of the big changes that were happening. "Hey!" I said. "Do you want to play a game with me or something?"

His eyes snapped open. "Why would I want to do that, exactly?"

"I don't know. Dodger always played with me, and I'm just kind of bored, so—"

"I am *not* bored, young William. I am tired. Although I know I look absolutely splendid for a six-thousand-year-old, even I need to get my beauty sleep. Plus, I have a brutal case of carpet-lag. And you will want me fresh in the morning, for when you are ready to make your third wish. Night-night, now!"

Wow, this guy had an attitude. But wait a minute: Wasn't he here to serve me? "Uh, excuse me, Lasorda?"

This time he only opened one eye. "Please do not bother me again until sunrise, William. And by the way, you may call me 'the Great Lasorda,' or, if you must, simply 'the Great.' But never 'Lasorda.'"

Okay, now I was getting annoyed. "Fine, then, the Great. Good night. And you can call me 'Master.'"

"I can, but rest assured I won't." And with that,

he closed his eyes for the last time and spun in midair to face the corner. Things weren't turning out quite as I had planned. I did my homework, read some comic books, drew some pictures of Babe Ruth playing ball with a chimp on my sketch pad, and went to the bathroom to brush my teeth and get ready for bed.

When my parents had said good night to me, I got myself all comfy under my covers and closed my eyes. And then I noticed a strange sound from the corner, like someone slowly cutting a piece of wood with a dull saw. Evidently, one of the things the Great Lasorda was great at was snoring.

In the morning when I woke up, the Great Lasorda was nowhere to be seen. For a few minutes, I tried to convince myself that the events of the day before had been a dream. In fact, while I was combing my hair in front of the mirror attached to the door of my closet, it even crossed my mind that everything that had happened since my last baseball game had been a dream. *Maybe I imagined Dodger,* I thought. *Maybe it's really just Sunday morning, and I'll go downstairs and get ready to play my second-to-last game of the season.*

There was a little brown speck on my reflection. I tried rubbing my cheek, but the speck wouldn't come off. *Duh,* I thought, *it's not on my face. It's on the mirror.* My heart raced a bit as I reached out to touch the smudge on the glass. It smeared off of the mirror and onto my finger. I held the finger under my nose and sniffed.

Chocolate, with a little sour milk mixed in.

Dodger hadn't been a dream. This was my life.

Downstairs, everyone was super-friendly and relaxed, which still struck me as unreal. I decided to try one more test, in case the part with Lasorda—sorry, the Great Lasorda—had been a dream. I got on my backpack with no coat—which I've always wanted to do—and grabbed a two-pack of Twinkies instead of my usual nutritious bag lunch. *Twinkies? I thought. Since when do we have Twinkies in the house?* Then I hugged my mom good-bye. She said, "No jacket, huh? Well, it is a glorious morning. And Twinkies for lunch? I suppose you deserve a nice treat after that wonderful dinner you made last night. Just don't make this a habit, okay?"

Then she turned me around and shoved me along on my way.

At the bus stop, I realized I was freezing. Lizzie came along and ignored me completely. I mean, she wasn't being angry or looking mean or anything. She just totally had no interest in my existence. I said, "Good morning, Lizzie."

She looked at me like we hadn't done this every morning for hundreds of school days in a row, and said, "Oh, I hadn't noticed you standing there. Good morning, uh, Will? That *is* your name, right?"

CHAPTER ELEVEN

Practice Makes Perfectly Confused

WOW, LIZZIE BARELY EVEN KNEW who I was. So my second wish had come true, too, exactly as I'd asked for it.

In class, I kept sneaking glances over at Lizzie every few minutes, expecting to catch her looking at me. But she never was. At lunch, I sat alone at my table for two and ate my Twinkies. That took about two minutes, and I spent the rest of the time watching Lizzie sitting and laughing with a couple of girls from another class. A kid walked by with a banana, and I thought of Dodger. I hoped he was eating better in the lamp than I was in my cafeteria. After nothing but Twinkies, I was starving.

The whole afternoon went the same way, except Lizzie started catching *me* looking at *her*. I could only imagine what she was thinking, but it was probably a lot like what I had always thought when Lizzie stared at me. Which was some pretty mean stuff. So, by three o'clock, I was completely freaking out. But I still had this tiny bit of—okay, I admit it—*hope* that Lizzie might not have forgotten *everything*. On the way to the bus stop, I sort of edged my way over to her and asked, "Hey, are you going to be at my game tomorrow?"

She looked completely mystified. "What game? What in the world are you talking about, and why are you talking about it to *me*?"

Well, that settled it. I couldn't sit through an entire bus ride with absolutely nobody who even noticed I was alive, so I decided that maybe walking home would clear my head. Usually my mom would be home on a Friday, and in my old life she would have had a cow if I hadn't gotten off the bus with Amy at the end of the day. I knew things would be different in my new life, though.

Walking past the Little League field didn't help to calm me down. I knew that there were only about twenty hours left until my big game, and I wished I had practiced more during the week. Before I had a chance to think too hard about it, I ran off the sidewalk and into the woods toward Dodger's magical field. I could sort of see where the blue carpet had been and followed the path until I got to the blue clearing. Strangely, the field was still there, but it was almost completely overgrown with weeds. The wooden backstop was half-rotted and leaned over at a crazy angle. The whole diamond looked like nobody had been there in twenty years.

Pretty spooky.

I would have given anything to be able to get some practice in before the game. I wished—

ZAP! As soon as the beginning of a wish formed in my head, the Great Lasorda appeared in front of me. "Good day, William. You summoned me?"

I nodded. I supposed that, without meaning to, I had summoned him.

"And are you ready to make your third wish?" He was so eager to be finished with me, he was practically rubbing his hands together with glee. But I knew I had to be really, really careful with my third wish.

"Not quite yet, the Great. Hey, while we're both here, how's about we play some ball?"

The Great Lasorda looked vaguely nauseous, like the thought of playing ball was just too sickening to even consider. But then a crafty little gleam appeared in his eye, and he waved his hand casually in the direction of the field. Instantly, it was back in tip-top shape. Next he wrinkled his nose at me, and I found myself in a full baseball uniform, complete with a very new, very stiff glove and really tight cleats. Finally, he held up his arms, and with a blinding flash, he was transported to the pitcher's mound, where he appeared in a flashy gold uniform that made him look like a cross between a major league baseball player and a circus clown.

Which seemed just about right.

I jogged onto the field, picked up a bat and batting helmet that were lying next to home plate, dropped my mitt, and stepped into the batter's box. As I dug my cleats into the dirt, I thought, *Wow, these things are tight*. Then the Great Lasorda wound up and pitched a bullet right down the middle. I gave a feeble swing, but my timing was way off. A new ball magically appeared in the Great Lasorda's hand, and he said, "You know, you could just wish to be a great baseball player. Honestly, you don't seem to have much going for you on the field, and your game *is* tomorrow. I always say, why *work* when you can *wish*?"

I gritted my teeth and said, "Just pitch the ball, Lasorda."

He snapped, "That's the *Great* Lasorda," and threw the exact same pitch in the exact same spot.

This time I was ready. I smacked the ball straight back at him. He ducked and gave a panicky little yelp as my line drive went screaming into center field. *Mr. Genie didn't look so great that time,* I thought.

After that, we settled into a rhythm. Ball after ball appeared in his hand, and each one came streaking to the plate. For some reason—maybe because I was so irritated with the Great Lasorda—I was hitting much better than usual. But after about twenty pitches, my heels were killing me.

The genie noticed. He walked about three-quarters of the way to home plate. With a sympathetic expression that made his face look like it was about to crack with the effort, he said, "Hey, I bet you wish those cleats were a little looser, don't you?"

"Yeah, I—" My mouth snapped shut in horror. "HEY! You tried to trick me into using up my wish, didn't you?"

He growled, "Just trying to make you comfortable, William," turned, and marched back to the mound.

After about ten more pitches, the Great Lasorda started rubbing at his pitching shoulder. "All right, William," he said. "I think it's time for us to work on your fielding." Then he waved one arm through the air and said, "Meet your new trainer: Rodger! Rodger is my most trusted assistant. He will take over now. I have had enough of this—this—manual labor! I am actually perspiring! Oh, the horror!" Suddenly, the Great Lasorda disappeared, and instantly reappeared at a table with a parasol over it, sipping some kind of pink slushy drink out of a coconut shell. I found myself standing at shortstop with the stiff glove on my left hand. Right where Lasorda had been, a blue chimp was at the plate holding a bat. For an instant, I thought it was Dodger. Then the chimp spoke, and I found out Dodger wasn't the only blue chimp in town.

"Hello, greetings, good day, *bonjour*!" he said. "I am Rodger, your friendly neighborhood Replacement On-call Dispatch Genie, Emergency Reserve."

This guy looked just like Dodger, only without the eye patch. Oh, and he was wearing a suit and tie, for some odd reason. I couldn't believe this. How could there be a replacement for Dodger? "Uh, didn't you forget the 'third class' part?"

The chimp looked down his nose at me like I had just insulted his mom. "Oh, William, please! I know that you are accustomed to working with my brother, Dodger. And, admittedly, Dodger is just about as third-class as they come. I assure you, however, that I am first-class all the way. First-class, top quality, pick of the litter—that's me! I understand that my poor, undistinguished brother caused you quite a bit of trouble. Well, you needn't have any worries about my performance or temperament. Despite any slight similarities in our appearances, we are opposites, antonyms, polar—"

I had to cut him off. First of all, I was getting mad. Just because Dodger had maybe fibbed a little and made a few mistakes didn't mean that his own brother should be talking trash about him while he was stuck in a bottle somewhere, unable to defend himself.

"Okay, I get it," I said through clenched teeth. "You're not Dodger. Now can we play ball?"

"Yes, sure, of course, absolutely. I am ready to hit the ball, smack it, give it a knock, pound it out. I think you will find me to be quite skillful, expert, masterful—"

"Uh, Rodger? Has anybody ever told you you talk funny? Why do you keep saying the same thing over and over?"

"Oh, I am sorry about the repetition, redundancy, the beating of a dead horse. It's just that I once spent several decades in a lamp with only a thesaurus to read, so sometimes—intermittently— now and again—that is to say, I occasionally find several ways to restate my point. Anyway, shall we get down to business, cut the chatter, skip the small talk?"

I wasn't sure exactly what he meant, but I nodded.

Suddenly Rodger was hitting balls in my direction. I barely got my glove up for the first one, a tough chopper right at me. I charged the ball, but it went about half an inch over the top of my glove and banged right off the bruise on my forehead.

"You have to get your glove higher, raise it, lift it up," Rodger shouted.

"Ooh," the Great Lasorda said. "Don't you wish the webbing on that glove were slightly bigger?"

"Nice try," I grunted. "Just keep hitting, Rodger."

"Is that a wish?" the genie asked.

"No, it's an order," I said.

The Great Lasorda smirked, and Rodger got ready to send another ball my way.

For someone wearing a suit and tie, Rodger was a shockingly hard hitter. At first, almost everything that came off his bat whacked off my shin, or bonked my chest, or bounced out of the brand-new glove. Watching from the sideline, the Great Lasorda offered several times to just make me a baseball star and be done with it. But the more the genie tried to make me quit, the more determined I was to stick it out. I imagined I had an eye patch on one eye and got back into my defensive stance.

Rodger was pretty chatty. As we played, he kept up a constant stream of synonym-filled advice. At first I started getting irritated, but then I thought, *Well, I'd be talking up a storm, too, if I'd just spent years and years all alone in a tiny space.* That made me feel kind of bad about sending Dodger back, so I tried to concentrate on my fielding.

Then, in the middle of a play, as if he had been reading my mind, Rodger said, "Don't worry about sending my brother back, by the way. This has been happening, going on, occurring for two thousand years. Dodger always hopes, wishes, believes that he will meet a client who values friendship over greed, but of course it never happens."

I got distracted wondering what Rodger meant, and the baseball whacked off the palm of my mitt and into the outfield. As I slipped off my glove, rubbed my bruised hand, and trudged into the grass to retrieve the ball, Rodger continued. "Poor Dodger, with his silly litter test. He really believes that just because someone picks up some trash, that makes the person special, exceptional, outstanding."

Hey, wait a minute, I thought. *The litter test works! Doesn't it? Well, except for Lizzie. Unless . . . well, unless Lizzie really* is *special.*

See, that's why you should never mix thinking with baseball. It's just too confusing. I threw the ball back to Rodger, and he smacked it back at me. Right when I was about to catch it on the fly, Rodger said, "I keep waiting for my brother to learn that every single human being on earth would always rather have three wishes than free him from his life of—"

I stopped in my tracks, and the baseball whizzed past my right ear into the grass. "What do you mean, free him? What do my three wishes have to do with—"

The Great Lasorda cut me off. "Rodger, William, I think that's quite enough chitchat out there. Now, get back to work! That is, unless William is ready to make his last wish."

We got back to work. In fact, Rodger made me go all the way out to right field and hit me a ton of long fly balls, until I could barely even see through all the sweat that was running down into my eyes. It was brutal, and it meant I was too far away to ask what he meant about freeing Dodger.

After maybe half an hour of nonstop fielding, I was starting to get a handle on the ball. I was also starting to get some hideous blisters on my glove hand and both feet. When the Great Lasorda finally told Rodger to call it a day, the chimp jogged all the way out to me and put one arm around my shoulder. His dress shirt had pulled up and out, so that when he raised his arm, I couldn't help but notice a flash of orange-and-white waistband sticking out from the top of his suit pants. Ha! It looked like Rodger and Dodger had something in common, after all. Rodger said, "Excellent practice, William! You really know how to work, struggle, grind it out, stick with it—"

I interrupted. I didn't have much time. "Rodger, what was that whole thing about greed and freeing Dodger?"

"Oh, I'm sure it's not my place to say. I can tell

you this, though, since you brought it up: Your friend Dodger had an argument with the Great Lasorda ages and ages ago. Dodger insisted that a human, a special human, would be willing to give up three wishes in exchange for one true friend. The genie said that no human would agree to give up even one wish just to get a friend. So they made a bet: If Dodger can find a person who is willing to give up a wish in order to have him as a friend, a buddy, a pal, an amigo—"

"Ahem," I said. We were getting pretty close to the Great Lasorda, who was giving me an intense glare.

Rodger looked startled. "Oh, sorry. If Dodger can find one person—one true-blue friend—who is willing to give up a wish in order to be his buddy, then the Great Lasorda has to set him free. As if *that* will ever happen."

"And if Dodger can't find a friend?"

"Then he must be banished over and over again, for all eternity."

I gulped.

The Great Lasorda snapped, "All right, enough of this little meeting, this powwow, this rendezvous, this—argh! I can't *stand* spending too much time with you, Rodger! Anyway, stop dilly-dallying and get over here!"

Rodger removed his arm from my shoulder and gave me one last look. It was like he was trying to send me a secret message with his eyes. Unfortunately, I don't speak chimp-eye, so I had no idea what the message was. Rodger looked away and started loping over to the Great Lasorda.

I trotted in behind him with gritted teeth. I would *not* show Lasorda how sore I was. I just wouldn't. As we all headed off the field, the genie said, "William, are you pleased with the assistance you received from Rodger today?"

"Yes, I am," I said.

"Good." He snapped his fingers. "Rodger, here is a nice banana for your efforts. Now, say goodbye to William."

"So long, farewell, *auf Wiedersehen*, good—"

The Great Lasorda snapped again, and Rodger was gone. The genie turned to me and said, "Well, that was surprisingly entertaining, wasn't it?"

"Yes, Your Greatness," I replied. But I was thinking, *Jeepers! What's with this guy and the sudden-banishing thing? Why can't he just let people hang out for a while?* And another part of my brain was saying, *Come on, Willie! Lasorda didn't banish Dodger—you did!*

The Great Lasorda sighed. "I don't suppose you'd like me to make you into a baseball superstar now, would you? Then I could just pop off into my hot tub for, oh, about a hundred years!"

I said, "No, I think I'll just see how things go with the game tomorrow. I can always make my wish in the middle of the game, right? So I guess we're stuck with each other until then."

He sighed again, much more loudly this time. Then he said, "Well, I suppose if I'm going to be stuck with you for another day, we might as well both be comfortable." With that, he waved his hand in a little circle. Suddenly, I was back in my street clothes, he was in his genie outfit, and we were standing in my backyard. And, flexing my arms and legs, I noticed my blisters and soreness were gone.

"Hey," I said. "Did you just—"

"Yes, I did," he said.

"Thanks," I replied.

He rolled his eyes. "Don't mention it. I'm serious—don't mention it. I have spent thousands of years building up my reputation for being firm with the humans I serve. I would hate it if word got around that I'm losing my edge. And now, farewell until the morning. I might not have a hundred years' worth of free time right now, but I can still squeeze in several hours in the hot tub before bed."

As soon as the Great Lasorda *POOF*ed his way out of there, I trudged inside the house. Even though my aches and pains were all gone, I was still totally exhausted. And, between the next day's game, Lizzie, Rodger, and Dodger's bet, I had way too much to think about. Somehow I got through dinner and a shower, but I could barely keep my eyes open long enough to brush my teeth and stagger to bed. My last thought before sleep overtook me was: *I only have one wish left, and I don't know what I want.*

CHAPTER TWELVE

Going Down Swinging

I HAD TO BE at the baseball field by noon. I woke up around ten with my usual pregame jitters, only today they were way worse than they had ever been before. Somehow I knew that the whole season would come down to me. I had no idea whether I could come through in the clutch without using up my last wish. And I felt a little bit like it would be cheating to beat out the rest of the league by magic. Plus—and I never would have believed this a week before—I found myself thinking it wouldn't be the same without Lizzie in the stands rooting for me, embarrassing cheers and all.

I spent the first half hour of my day lying in bed trying to get a handle on all of these thoughts that were tumbling around in my head. Eventually I realized that I couldn't solve my problems without getting up and facing the day, so I went to the bathroom, got dressed in my baseball uniform, and headed downstairs for breakfast. My parents and Amy had already eaten, but they were still hanging around the dining room table. Mom was reading the newspaper, and Dad was looking over a letter from the editor of his newest book: *My Marriage Is Perfect: What's Next?* He turned to my mom and said, "I can't believe this! My editor says we have to change the title!"

Without looking up, Mom asked, "Why, dear?"

"He says nobody is going to believe a book called *My Marriage Is Perfect.* And he thinks all my fans will want to know when I started writing fiction!"

Meanwhile, Amy was getting ready to make me feel sick.

I got myself a bowl of instant oatmeal and sat down. "So," Amy said cheerfully, "today's your big game, huh? I bet you'll hit a home run. Or maybe two."

I tried hard to smile at her.

She continued. "On the other hand, maybe you'll get hit by a pitch. Maybe it'll get you right in the forehead. Maybe the pitcher will get confused and aim right for the old plus sign—did you notice it's turning yellow and green now? And maybe your helmet will fall off at just the right moment. And when the ball nails you right on the cranium—cranium, right? We're learning bones this week in school!—maybe your brains will start to dribble out your ear. Actually, it'll prob'ly look a lot like your oatmeal. Did you know brains are gray? And mushy. And they float around in your head. I mean, unless they're coming out your—"

"MOM!" I shouted. "Can you please make her stop?"

"Dear," my mother said, "you know we don't like to interfere when you kids are expressing yourselves."

What? She had always LOVED to interfere when we kids were expressing ourselves. Jeepers, one stupid wish, and suddenly it was like I was living with Martians.

After I finally managed to choke down my

oatmeal—which did kind of look like brains, actually—I had a crazy idea. Maybe I could call Lizzie and ask her to come to my game. I mean, I had never called her or anything, even before she totally forgot she knew me. Come to think of it, I had never even called a girl on the phone. But her number would be in the school directory. And I couldn't help thinking that the old Lizzie wouldn't have wanted to miss my last game, especially after our big practice and everything. Plus, I just kept remembering how she had helped me with that major, hideous nosebleed. I tried to imagine my old pal Tim doing that, but there was no way: He would have just said, "Oh, man, I'm not touching your nose!" Or he would have run all the way home gagging.

Holy moley. It was almost like, for a little while there, Lizzie had been a real friend. Without giving myself any more time to think, I raced upstairs, grabbed the school directory from the side of my parents' bed, found her number, and dialed. My hand sweated all over the phone as I listened to her phone ringing. One ring . . . two . . . three . . . four . . . Then her machine picked up.

Oh, boy. I hate talking to answering machines! But at least I didn't have to talk to Lizzie's parents. Or Lizzie, come to think of it. When the beep came, I found myself talking really, really fast: "Hi, Lizzie, this is Willie. From your class. I was just, uh, wondering whether you might want to come to my baseball game today. It's at twelve-thirty. It's a pretty big deal. Uh, I mean, if we win, we'll be the champions of the league. It's at the field." I paused to smack myself on the forehead. What was I saying? *It's at the field.* I was a moron. Where would she think it was: on the lake? "And, uh, I'd be really happy to see you there." I hung up, and then I heard a little giggle behind me. Amy was standing there.

"Ooohhh, Willie likes a girl! Willie likes a g-uuurrrr-uuulllll! Mom, guess what? Willie—"

I clamped my hand over her mouth. "Shut *up!*" I hissed.

She nodded. When I let go, she said, "Well, it's true. You *do* like a girl."

I said, "I do *not* like a girl. I just asked Lizzie if she wanted to come to my game."

"I know," Amy said. "So you asked her out. It's like a *date*."

"No, it's not."

"Well, that's what Lizzie is going to think. Wow, an English girl. You have an *international* date!" She burst into a giggle fit again and ran out of the room.

I was horrified. I grabbed the phone again and hit redial. This time the machine picked up after only one ring. As soon as I heard the *BEEP*, I said, "Uh, it's not a date or anything. I mean, I'm not, like, asking you out. You're nice and everything, but—" Jeepers, I had no idea what to say. Then I realized I hadn't even said my name. "Uh, this is Willie again. By the way."

Then I hung up. I heard a shuffling noise behind me. Amy had snuck back into the room. She had both hands on her mouth and was clearly trying to hold back a massive explosion of giggles. As I pushed past her, she said, "This is Willie again. By the way!" Then she doubled over, laughing.

I got my cleats and my mitt as fast as I could, then rushed out of the house. Why stay home and embarrass myself when I was so good at doing that at the ball field? I decided to cut through the forest. Now that I knew the way, I felt pretty comfortable in there. I thought about Dodger. I wondered what he was up to. If the lamp had transformed itself again, who knew where he was or what was happening to him? For all I knew, it had turned into a pizza box, and he was all bent over sideways with a lump of cold cheese stuck to his head.

But that was his own fault, right? *He* had messed everything up, not me. And he had lied to me. Well, not lied, exactly. But he hadn't told me the whole truth, either.

On the other hand, we had kind of had a good time together. I mean, when he wasn't injuring me, getting me in trouble, or destroying my house.

But he couldn't grant me any wishes.

But my wishes were turning out all weird.

But, but, but. It was all so confusing. I wished—

POOF! Oh, no. I had summoned the Great Lasorda. He grinned hugely at me, showing what looked like an endless ocean of perfect white teeth. "William," he intoned, "are you ready for me to make you a star?"

"Well," I replied, "why don't you just stick around and we can see how the game goes, okay?"

His smile disappeared, and he started muttering under his breath about wishy-washy humans who didn't even know what they wanted. He stayed, though.

At the field, there were already a couple of guys from my team warming up. I said, "Hey, dudes!" They ignored me completely, except for the guy I had stranded on third base the week before. "Hey, Wimpy. I was kind of hoping you'd be home sick today. But since you're here, do you wanna play right field for a while?"

As I trudged out to right field, the Great Lasorda whispered in my ear, "A star, William. Just say the word!"

We warmed up for a while. Or the rest of the team warmed up. I just stood there in right field, where the balls never go, and scanned the crowd. No Lizzie. About ten minutes before game time, my parents and Amy appeared. But that wasn't quite the same thing. Besides, my parents had changed so much, I almost didn't even recognize them. And as far as I was concerned, Amy hadn't changed enough.

Looking at my parents gave me an idea. I mumbled under my breath, "I wish . . ."

Just as I had hoped, the Great Lasorda appeared next to me. He was chowing down on one of the greasy hot dogs from the snack stand. I tried to sound all casual as I asked, "Hey, the Great, can I ask you for a favor? Not a wish, but a favor?"

He considered this for a moment, then said, "I can't promise anything, but I will listen. Just make it snappy. I'm dying for some french fries!"

"Um, I was just wondering whether you could maybe adjust my first two wishes a little."

"Adjust them? Why in the world would I adjust the results of your wishes? That would be like admitting I might have made a mistake. And the Great Lasorda never, ever makes mistakes."

"No," I admitted. "You didn't make any mistake at all—you did exactly what I asked for. But it turns out that what I asked for and what I really needed aren't the same thing."

He stroked his chin in some sort of wise-man

gesture. Or maybe he was just checking for ketchup. Then he said, "Speak to me. I will consider your request while I am enjoying the second course of my snack-bar feast. I haven't eaten anything this deliciously greasy since the Greek health inspectors closed down the funnel-cake stand at the first Olympics!"

Quickly, in the last moments before game time, I told the genie what I wanted. Then my team's coaches waved us into the dugout, the umpire shouted, "Play ball!" and the Great Lasorda got himself an order of fries.

The first two innings were uneventful. In right field, I had nothing to do but slap at mosquitoes and look through the crowd for Lizzie. Both teams were held scoreless, and my team didn't even have a hit going into the third. As usual, I was batting ninth, so I got up in the bottom of the inning with a guy on second and one out. Incredibly, with two strikes, the pitcher served me up a total meatball. The pitch was straight over the heart of the plate, moving too slowly to be a fastball but too quickly to be a decent change-up. I thought, *I can hit this!* I swung, and the bat met the ball with a sharp *CRACK!* It was my first-ever line drive. Unfortunately, the ball went screaming straight into the second baseman's mitt. The runner had taken off as soon as I hit the ball, so all the second baseman had to do was step on the bag for the force-out.

Perfect, I thought. *The first time I hit a ball hard, and it's an inning-ending double play.*

As I started my long, sad walk out to right field, the Great Lasorda appeared next to me again. Through a huge mouthful of cotton candy, he said, "William, just say the word and you'll be in home-run city!"

"Not yet," I said. "I smacked that ball. I can do this without magic! But what about my request? You know, adjusting the first two wishes?"

He rolled his eyes and gestured to the stands. My heart jumped in my chest. Lizzie was sitting on the bleachers. When she saw me, she waved and shouted, "Hi, Willie!" But she didn't cheer. This was excellent!

"Thanks, the Great," I said. "That takes care of Lizzie. And how about the other adjustment I asked for?"

"You'll see," he said mysteriously.

The next three innings were scoreless for both teams, and we only got one more hit that whole time. Needless to say, the hit didn't come from me. I came to bat in the bottom of the sixth, and actually made contact again. This time, though, it was just a weak pop-up about two feet in front of home plate. The catcher caught the ball, and for the second time I found myself walking out to right field next to an increasingly well-fed genie. Once more, he told me he could make me a star. Once more I told him I wasn't ready to use my third wish for that yet. Once more he *POOF*ed his way back to the snack bar.

In the top of the seventh, with one out, our pitcher suddenly straightened up after a pitch and grabbed his arm in pain. The coach replaced him with our only other pitcher, who is nowhere near as good. In no time at all, the other team scored three runs. We finally retired a couple of their batters, mostly through luck, but the damage was done. Now we had just one half-inning to score three or more runs, when we hadn't even managed to score once in the first six.

You might have noticed by now that whenever there's a chance in my life for things to get as complicated as possible, that's exactly what happens. So of course my team immediately got two outs, and then loaded the bases just in time for me to once again be the last batter of the game. I mean, you could say, "What are the chances?" But really, by the time you have your own personal genie and your best friend in the world is a banished chimpanzee, I'm pretty sure that the odds have basically flown out the window.

Oh, wow. It hit me as I stepped into the batter's box: *My best friend in the world is a banished chimpanzee.*

I knew my third wish!

I thought as hard as I could: *I wish . . .* Nothing happened. I looked around: No genie in sight. And while I was looking around, the pitcher blew a fastball by, right under my chin. "Be careful, Willie!" my mother shouted. The next pitch looked like it was coming right at me. I stepped back, but the umpire called it a strike. "Not *that* careful!" my mom yelled. Several people in the crowd laughed, but I was happy. I wasn't sure where the heck the Great Lasorda had gone, but clearly, he had taken care of readjusting my mom before disappearing.

While I was thinking about that, the pitcher blew another fastball by me. The count was one ball, two strikes. It was basically now or never. I tried to summon the genie again: *I wish . . .* He didn't appear. The next ball was *way* outside. Ball two. I swung at the next pitch and fouled it off. The count remained at 2–2. The pitcher must have thought I was a complete sucker, because he threw the next one in the dirt, thinking I'd lunge for it and end the game with a superlame strike-out. A week before, he would have been right. But now I didn't fall for the trick, and the count was three balls and two strikes.

I asked the umpire for a time-out, stepped out of the box, and turned my back on home plate. Well, now the season was completely on my shoulders. The next pitch would decide everything. Every kid in our dugout was yelling. Every single person in the stands was standing up and yelling. Even the coaches were shaking the chain-link fence. I bent over, put my hands on my knees, and took a deep breath. I didn't know where the Great Lasorda had gone, but it looked like I was on my own.

So as soon as I thought that, of course he appeared. "Sorry," he said, wiping his mouth with the back of one greasy hand. "I was in line for some popcorn and I didn't want to lose my spot. So *now* are you ready for your third wish?"

Even with all of the insanity going on around me, I smiled. "Yes, I am," I said.

I really was ready. I looked up in the stands at my family. I snuck a glance at Lizzie. I looked at the pitcher and realized I wasn't scared anymore. And I knew for sure that my third wish would be the right one. I took a deep breath and spoke.

"I wish I had Dodger back!"

The Great Lasorda stepped back in shock, then let out a huge burp. "Excuse me," he said. "But did I just hear you say that your last wish is to have *Dodger* back?"

I nodded.

"*Dodger?*" he repeated. "Dodger, the blue chimpanzee?"

"Yes, that's the Dodger I mean," I said.

"Are you *sure*?" he asked. "No second thoughts? No adjustments?"

"No second thoughts. No adjustments," I replied.

The umpire tapped me on the shoulder and said, "It's time to get back in the box, kid."

I turned away from the Great Lasorda and stepped back into the batter's box. Just then, Dodger appeared. He was leaning against the backstop, looking straight across the plate at me. There was a slice of pepperoni stuck to his shoulder. "Dude," he said, "it's about time! I was starting to think you'd *never* ask for me back!" He picked the pepperoni out of his fur, flipped it up in the air, and caught it in his mouth. He swallowed with a gulp, gave me a huge, toothy smile, and said, "So what are you waiting for? Hit that thing out of here so we can go have a party, a fiesta, a night on the town!"

Wow, it was great to have my buddy back. But had he just said the same thing, three different ways? For a second he had almost sounded like—

Nah, it couldn't be. It just couldn't be.

I shook my head to clear my thoughts and took

a last quick look around. My parents were smiling encouragingly. Amy was grinning, too. Behind Dodger's left shoulder, Lizzie was leaning forward in her seat. Could she still see him? I wasn't sure, but from where she was sitting, she definitely couldn't see the thumbs-up sign he gave me. Even with all the pressure of the moment, I could feel joy spreading through my whole body. It felt like I had the greatest secret in the world. And do you know what? I did.

I tapped my bat on home plate, then wagged it menacingly at the pitcher. He gave me the evil eye.

The umpire shouted, "PLAY BALL!"

Go Fish!

GOFISH

JORDAN SONNENBLICK

What did you want to be when you grew up?
I wanted to be some combination of writer, teacher, and drummer. I never really thought I'd end up doing all three, though.

When did you realize you wanted to be a writer?
I don't remember exactly, but it was really, really early in life. However, I spent the first thirty-three years of my life bragging about how I was going to write a book someday, instead of actually working on my writing!

What's your first childhood memory?
Some kid named Anthony from down the block threw sand in my eyes, and my Grampa Sol sang the Sandman Song to me until I calmed down and fell asleep. I just remember feeling so completely safe once I was all snuggled up with Grampa.

What's your most embarrassing childhood memory?
My eyes are terrible without my glasses on. Once at sleepaway camp when I was thirteen, I was showing off while waterskiing. In the middle of doing tricks on one ski, I crashed into a fifteen-foot-long wooden float. Afterward, I couldn't walk right for days!

What's your favorite childhood memory?
Watching the 1977 and 1978 World Series with my dad (The Yankees beat the Dodgers twice in a row!). Or when my parents got me my first drum set.

As a young person, who did you look up to most?
My Grampa Sol. He was a teacher and author, which drove me to pursue those careers as well. Also, he was the one person who never, ever lied to me. In my experience, kids appreciate honesty above nearly any other character trait.

What was your worst subject in school?
Sitting still. Come to think of it, that's still my worst subject.

What was your best subject in school?
Either English, or making my friends laugh. I haven't changed much, apparently.

What was your first job?
All through high school, I was both a tutor and a summer camp counselor. If you ever need help with algebra or archery, I'm your guy.

How did you celebrate publishing your first book?
With a big party in my backyard—a tent, catering, and even a wiffleball game. Then my original publisher went out of business three days later. Yikes!

Where do you write your books?
Mostly at the computer in my kitchen, but sometimes on a laptop wherever I happen to be. As long as I have headphones with me, I'm pretty good at shutting out the world in order to write.

Where do you find inspiration for your writing?
From kids. My book ideas always start with a kid doing something that puzzles or amazes me. The Dodger books, for example, are inspired by events in my son's real life. No, he doesn't have a blue chimp for a best friend, but he does have many of the same worries and challenges Willie does.

Which of your characters is most like you?
Oh, gosh, ALL of them. No one character is 100% me, but each has big chunks of my personality, habits, strengths, and weaknesses. People who know me really well always say they can hear my voice in the words of each of my main characters.

When you finish a book, who reads it first?
My wife. In fact, she reads my pages daily while I'm writing every first draft. She's also the only person in the world whose judgment I never, ever ignore—which makes both my writing and my marriage better!

Are you a morning person or a night owl?
Both; I just need a nap in the middle of the day. I always tell my wife I should move to Spain so everyone around me would be taking a daily siesta, too.

What's your idea of the best meal ever?
My last Thanksgiving with my Dad. I wish we could have had a hundred more just like it.

Which do you like better: cats or dogs?
Neither—I'm completely allergic! Well, that's not quite fair. I like dogs a lot, even if I don't like the itchy welts I get if I play with one for more than three minutes.

What do you value most in your friends?
Loyalty.

Where do you go for peace and quiet?
Anyplace where I can play an instrument or read. I also really
like riding my bicycle out in the country where there's no traffic.
In fact, whenever I get stuck in the middle of my writing, I find
that a long bike ride is a great way to clear the jam and get my
brain working again.

What makes you laugh out loud?
Just about anything. I laugh a lot.

What's your favorite song?
Just about anything the Beatles ever wrote. In fact, I love the Beatles so much that when each of my children was born, I made
sure the Beatles album *Abbey Road* was the first music they
heard.

Who is your favorite fictional character?
Probably Hagrid, from Harry Potter. He has such loyalty, and
such a huge, brave heart.

What are you most afraid of?
Failing to come through for the people I love.

What time of year do you like best?
Baseball season. I spend the whole winter looking forward to
the spring, when I can start pitching batting practice to my son
and his friends again. Incidentally, I throw a pretty good two-
seam fastball, a decent curve, and a killer cut fastball.

What's your favorite TV show?
I don't really have one. I guess my default answer would be any televised Yankees game.

If you were stranded on a desert island, who would you want for company?
My family. Or anyone who was good at shipbuilding.

If you could travel in time, where would you go?
Back to my old summer camp in the Poconos, around 1985. Or to the moment when either of my kids was born—there's just nothing else like becoming a parent.

What's the best advice you have ever received about writing?
If you want to get better at writing, you'd better read a lot. Most other writing advice is basically a matter of taste or opinion, but the connection between reading and good writing is a 100% non-negotiable fact. If I could, I'd carve this piece of advice above the doorway of every school in America.

What do you want readers to remember about your books?
I don't really think about what I'd like them to remember, but I hope that while they're reading, they come to care about my characters as much as I do.

What would you do if you ever stopped writing?
Go back to teaching. I really miss my old students. The great thing about working with middle schoolers is that no two days are ever the same, and I miss having that kind of fun randomness in my daily life.

What do you like best about yourself?
My thick, lustrous hair. Just kidding! Really, I am proud that I am
kind, and that I try my best to make other people's lives easier.
But I do, in fact, have thick and lustrous hair. ☺

What is your worst habit?
Self-criticism.

What is your best habit?
I dunno, probably my addiction to reading.

**What do you consider to be your greatest
accomplishment?**
Fatherhood.

Where in the world do you feel most at home?
At home. Or in NYC, Houston, Philly, or London. It's funny: I like
big cities a lot—but being in my quiet little house with my family
is better.

What do you wish you could do better?
Play guitar. I'm an okay player, but I am terrible about practicing.

**What would your readers be most surprised to learn
about you?**
Maybe that I love to cook, but hate using recipes?

Keep reading for an excerpt from

Jordon Sonnenblick's **Dodger for President**,

coming soon in hardcover from Feiwel and Friends.

EXCERPT

"Dude!" Dodger shouted as he jumped into my arms.

"Oww!" I yelped as we tumbled together to the floor of my room. This happened pretty often, because I was a wimpy, 80-pound fifth grader and Dodger was a really strong, 125-pound chimp. With blue fur. And bright orange-and-white surfer shorts. Plus an eye patch.

Oh, and he's invisible to everyone except me and this girl named Lizzie.

It's a really long story.

But the point is, Dodger knocked me over and landed right on top of me. It's amazing how pointy a chimpanzee's elbows are. So as I was lying there, gasping for air, Dodger started talking a mile a minute. The conversation went like this:

DODGER: Dude, you missed so much while you were in Cleveland with your dad!

ME: *Gasp . . .*

DODGER: Lizzie took me to school, just like we planned. And there was just one little problem.

ME: *Gasp* . . .

DODGER: Like, there was this science quiz. It was totally hard. There were all these, um, questions and stuff. And you had to fill in these little bubbles with letters next to them, but I really didn't see what the letters had to do with the questions. The question would be all *What type of rock is made when a volcano erupts and then the lava cools?* But the answers would be all like *A.* Or *B.* Or *C.* Or even *D.* Dude, I don't know a whole lot about rocks, but even a chimp knows there's no kind of rock called "A Rock." 'Cause that would be just completely confusing. Somebody would ask you, "What do you call that cool rock you're holding?" And you'd go, "This? It's called 'A Rock.'" And they'd go, "Yeah, I know it's a rock. But what kind of rock is it?" Then you'd be all, "Buddy, the *name* of this rock is 'A Rock.'" And they'd be all, "Why do you have to be such a wise guy? All I did was ask the name of a rock." So you'd go, "Exactly!" And then they'd probably hit you or something.

But, you know, I did my best for you.

ME: What do you mean, you . . . *gasp* . . . did your "best" for me?

DODGER: Well, I didn't want you to get all behind in your work, right? So I just wrote your name on top of a quiz and tried really hard to fill in all the bubbles.

ME: Okay, so you took a test in my name, on a day when I wasn't even in school. I guess that was the problem.

DODGER: Uh, no, that wasn't the problem. I mean, I made this really great sentence out of all the letters. Do you want to hear it?

ME (*puts head in hands*): *Gasp* . . . sure.

DODGER: Okay, here it is: "CAB! A CAB! DAD, A CAB! A . . . A . . . BAD CAB!" See, it's like this little story about you and your dad. Get it? You, like, see this taxicab, right? So you yell to your dad, and you try to get the driver to stop. But the cab just keeps going. Genius, huh?

ME: *Groan* . . .

DODGER: I still don't get the part about the rocks, though. Well, maybe we'll get a lot of points for creativity.

You couldn't leave this chimp alone for a minute. So apparently a whole weekend plus a school day were completely out of the question. I got up off the floor, checked myself for broken ribs, and dusted off. Meanwhile Dodger started to tell me about the rest of his day at school. It was hard to believe there was more, but I hadn't even heard about the problem yet.

"So then in social studies, they're learning about how all these explorer guys discovered North America and discovered South America and, like, discovered Africa. I totally wanted to set the record straight, but I didn't."

Well, that was a relief. "Uh, Dodger, what did you want to set the record straight about, exactly?"

"I wanted to tell them about how chimpanzees had already totally conquered all those places, thousands and thousands of years ago. Like before you called it South America, we called it Banana World. And before you had Europe, we had No-Monkeys-Land."

I always get drawn in when he does this. I don't know why, but it happens every stupid time. So I said, "What about Asia?"

He smirked. "Chimptopia, of course."

"Africa?"

"Land O'Mammals."

"New Jersey?"

Dodger made a horrified face. "Dude, who would want to conquer New Jersey? Anyway, you would have been proud of me, Willie. I didn't say a single word. Well, okay, I kind of laughed when the cake fell on James Beeks."

"Wait a minute, a cake fell on James Beeks? Was *that* the problem?"

" 'Problem'? It was awesome. I mean, there was this huge, brown-and-orange volcano cake on the ledge over the chalkboard. And, you know, Beeks is the coolest kid in the school, right? And he always calls you Wimpy and says you're a total dork, right? So I just thought it was funny when he got . . ."

"What do you mean, a total dork?" I blurted.

Dodger looked sheepish for a moment. "Well, you know, not a dork, exactly. It's not your fault about your little dressing-funny problem, since your mom picks out all your clothes, right? Plus, who can blame you for not having any guy friends since Tim moved away? It's hard to hang out with the guys if you're not good at—oh, never mind."

I was insulted, but I forced myself to take a deep breath. The madder I got, the more off topic Dodger got, and I had a feeling I would really need to know what the mysterious problem was. "Whatever. So how did the cake fall on James Beeks anyway?"

"Okay, you know how I was trying not to say anything about the whole social studies thing? That was totally hard for me, right? So I was just kind of hopping up and down in my seat next to Lizzie. I guess that made the ledge over the chalkboard vibrate. And the cake just slid off the ledge. Then Mrs. Starsky tried to make a jumping catch. It was pretty awesome, but she fumbled the cake. So it bounced off her hands onto James's head, upside down."

I could just tell there had to be more to this story, so I waited. Sure enough, Dodger continued, "I don't know why he got so mad. I only laughed a little. And it's not like my laugh really sounds like Lizzie's anyway. But he thought Lizzie was laughing at him—I guess he couldn't hear that well through all the cake around his ears. So he got all mad, and Mrs. Starsky yelled at Lizzie."

"Oh," I said. "I guess that's the problem, huh?"

"No," Dodger replied. "That's not the problem. So then Lizzie started yelling at James, right? And, dude, he was getting completely heated. He kept trying to wipe all this orange icing off his face and yelling back at her. Then Mrs. Starsky was standing between James and Lizzie, trying to see if James was okay, even though it was only a cake that fell on him in the first place. It was really funny, but I only laughed a little bit more. So the teacher thought it was Craig Flynn, 'cause he usually laughs at everybody, right?"

This was getting better and better. *Not!* I thought I heard our doorbell ringing downstairs, but I wasn't going to go down and miss the end of this story. My mom could get the door.

"Everybody was going totally bananas. I mean, you know I love bananas, but—I mean, everyone was going nuts—well, I like nuts, too, but you know what I mean. Lizzie and James were yelling at each other; Mrs. Starsky was yelling at Craig; and Craig was just standing there totally confused and wondering who he should blame for the whole thing so he could beat them up at lunch recess. Then somehow it wound up that Craig, Mrs. Starsky, and James were all looking right at Lizzie."

Wow. "So that was the problem, huh?"

"Nope," said Dodger. Just then, I heard footsteps charging up the stairs. Dodger looked at my bedroom door and gulped. "The problem—and it's really just a teeny little problem. I mean fifth grade isn't really a very long part of your life span, when you think about it." Dodger swallowed again and said, "The problem is—"

Lizzie burst into the room, causing the door to bang off the wall. She was out of breath, but she immediately said, "Dodger, did you tell Willie about the class election?"

I looked at Dodger. Lizzie saw my confused face, then glared at Dodger. I said, "Election?"

Dodger looked like he was going to throw up. "Dude," he said, "*that's* the problem!"

ALSO AVAILABLE
FROM SQUARE FISH BOOKS

If you like sports, you'll love these SQUARE FISH sports books!

Airball · L. D. Harkrader
ISBN-13: 978-0-312-37382-5 · $6.99 U.S./$7.99 Can.
"Even non-basketball fans will savor the on-court action and will cheer loudly for these determined players." —*Publishers Weekly*

Busted! · Betty Hicks
ISBN-13: 978-0-312-38053-3 · $6.99 U.S./$7.99 Can.
"Soccer fans will appreciate the exciting game action....A winning combination of sports and humor." —*School Library Journal*

Getting in the Game · Dawn FitzGerald
ISBN-13: 978-0-312-37753-3 · $6.99 U.S./$8.99 Can.
"Fast and funny...and readers who are caught up by the sports will stay around for the family and friendship drama." —*Booklist*

Soccer Chick Rules · Dawn FitzGerald
ISBN-13: 978-0-312-37662-8 · $6.99 U.S./$8.99 Can.
"An expression of the sheer joy of athletic competition and the hard-breathing fray of the game." —*Kirkus Reviews*